“Give

that love

He looked half hopeful that she could and half certain that she couldn’t.

Carolyn’s mind spun around in circles. How could she ever convince him when he didn’t want to be convinced? “What about poetry? Could anyone who wasn’t in love have written ‘How do I love thee, let me count the ways…’ or classic love songs?”

“Is that the best you can do?” he asked. “Come up with poetry and love songs? Those are cruel travesties, written to make money for the composers, to mislead innocent people into thinking they are in love.”

“Don’t you think you’re being too pessimistic?” she asked.

“No. I think I’m being realistic. But if I did fall in love, Carolyn, it would be with someone like you. You’re everything I admire in a woman. Everything I want….”

But not a woman he could ever have.

VIRGIN BRIDES

Celebrate the joys of first love with unforgettable stories by your most beloved authors.

Dear Reader,

As senior editor for the Silhouette Romance line, I'm lucky enough to get first peek at the stories we offer you each month. Each editor searches for stories with an emotional impact, that make us laugh or cry or feel tenderness and hope for a loving future. And we do this with *you,* the reader, in mind. We hope you continue to enjoy the variety each month as we take you from first love to forever....

Susan Meier's wonderful story of a hardworking single mom and the man who sweeps her off her feet is *Cinderella and the CEO.* In *The Boss's Baby Mistake*, Raye Morgan tells of a heroine who accidentally gets inseminated with her new boss's child! The fantasy stays alive with Carol Grace's *Fit for a Sheik* as a wedding planner's new client is more than she bargained for....

Valerie Parv always creates a strong alpha hero. In *Booties and the Beast*, Sam's the strong yet tender man. Julianna Morris's lighthearted yet emotional story *Meeting Megan Again* reunites two people who only *seem* mismatched. And finally Carolyn Greene's *An Eligible Bachelor* has a very special secondary character—along with a delightful hero and heroine!

Next month, look for our newest ROYALLY WED series with Stella Bagwell's *The Expectant Princess*. Marie Ferrarella astounds readers with *Rough Around the Edges*—her 100th title for Silhouette Books! And, of course, there will be more stories throughout the year chosen just for you.

Happy reading!

Mary-Theresa Hussey

Mary-Theresa Hussey
Senior Editor

Please address questions and book requests to:
Silhouette Reader Service
U.S.: 3010 Walden Ave., P.O. Box 1325, Buffalo, NY 14269
Canadian: P.O. Box 609, Fort Erie, Ont. L2A 5X3

Fit for a Sheik

CAROL GRACE

Published by Silhouette Books
America's Publisher of Contemporary Romance

ISBN 0-373-19500-1

FIT FOR A SHEIK

This edition published by arrangement with Harlequin Books S.A.

Visit Silhouette at www.eHarlequin.com

Printed in U.S.A.

Books by Carol Grace

Silhouette Romance

Make Room for Nanny #690
A Taste of Heaven #751
Home Is Where the Heart Is #882
Mail-Order Male #955
The Lady Wore Spurs #1010
**Lonely Millionaire* #1057
**Almost a Husband* #1105
**Almost Married* #1142
The Rancher and the Lost Bride #1153
†*Granted: Big Sky Groom* #1277
†*Granted: Wild West Bride* #1303
†*Granted: A Family for Baby* #1345
Married to the Sheik #1391
The Librarian's Secret Wish #1473
Fit for a Sheik #1500

*Miramar Inn
†Best-Kept Wishes

Silhouette Desire

Wife for a Night #1118
The Heiress Inherits a Cowboy #1145
Expecting... #1205
The Magnificent M.D. #1277

CAROL GRACE

has always been interested in travel and living abroad. She spent her junior year in college in France and toured the world working on the hospital ship *HOPE.* She and her husband spent the first year and a half of their marriage in Iran, where they both taught English. She has studied Arabic and Persian languages. Then, with their toddler daughter, they lived in Algeria for two years.

Carol says that writing is another way of making her life exciting. Her office is her mountaintop home, which overlooks the Pacific Ocean and which she shares with her inventor husband, their daughter, who just graduated college, and their teenage son.

Dear Reader,

It's a special pleasure to write a story about a virgin bride. Especially a bride who has purposely saved herself for marriage, who waits as long as it takes to give herself to that one special man—the love of her life, her groom, her husband. While all around her women are engaging in casual sex, the virgin bride holds off, knowing that somewhere there will be a man who will walk into her life, fall in love with her and walk down the aisle with her. Together they'll discover the joys and ecstasy of physical love that come with a committed relationship—marriage. The virgin bride knows she's made the right decision. Whether she marries a sheik, a cowboy, a CEO or the man next door, she comes to him as pure as the white dress she's wearing, his virgin bride.

Carol Grace

Chapter One

The late spring rain beat down against the window of the bridal shop, I DO! I DO!, but inside it was all white satin, pink roses and plaster of Paris wedding cakes. Carolyn Evans sat behind her desk facing her clients, a young couple who'd come to the wedding consultant to help them plan the "perfect wedding." Of course there was no such thing. There was always something—the ring bearer who tripped as he ran down the aisle and burst into tears, the forgotten boutonniere, the best man's risqué toast, the band that played too loudly or too softly. But one could always dream, always hope, as she did...if not for the perfect wedding, for the perfect groom. But that's all it was so far—just a dream.

Out of the corner of her eye, Carolyn saw a strange man in a dark suit standing outside in front of her window—in the rain—staring in at her. She gave a tiny shiver of apprehension. Was it possible he was a disgruntled suitor out for revenge? No, of course not. She was being ridiculous, letting her imagination run away with her. It was just the rain, the lateness of the hour and her fatigue after a long day of heading off minor disasters like bridesmaid dresses in the wrong color and an irate mother-of-the-bride. The man was most likely a prospective groom, sizing her up, trying to decide if she was up to planning his wedding or trying to decide whether to get married at all. She prided herself on being able to calm both jittery brides and grooms. She gave him a quick, reassuring smile and turned her attention back to the couple.

"At some point in the ceremony," the groom on the other side of her desk said, "I want to present Melinda with a rock as the emperor penguins of the Antarctic do in their courtship ritual. Will that be a problem?"

"No problem at all," Carolyn assured him. No more problem than the hot-air balloon wedding she'd arranged or the underwater ceremony for the professional divers. "I'm here to help you plan a wedding that may not be perfect, but one with your own personal stamp on it. I've never seen a ceremony with a penguin rock-giving exchange, but I don't see why..."

The mysterious stranger in the Armani suit chose that moment to enter the shop. Probably tired of the rain falling on his broad shoulders. All three heads turned in his direction.

"Ms. Evans?" he asked in a voice that matched his appearance. Strong, deep and virile.

"Yes, I'll be with you in a moment," she said, noting that the rain had barely dampened his Italian-tailored suit or his crisp dark hair. He looked like he'd just stepped out of *GQ*. Something told her he always looked that way, rain or shine.

"I can't wait a moment," he said, looming behind the

couple at the desk. "I must see you now." His look was arrogant, his tone was insistent.

Taken aback by this unexpected aggressive approach, Carolyn stood and glared at him. The bride-to-be's mouth fell open in surprise and her groom's eyes widened.

"If you don't mind..." Carolyn began. But it was clear he *did* mind. With a hasty glance over their shoulders at the intruder, the young couple grabbed a handful of brochures from the desk and started for the door.

"We'll come back when you have more time," Melinda said.

"When you're not busy," her groom added before he shut the door behind him.

"That's better," the man said. "Now we can get down to business."

"You interrupted us," she said sternly. "They had an appointment and you don't."

"They can come back another time. I can't. I'm a busy man."

Carolyn choked back a protest that other people were equally busy but they had the time to make and keep their appointments.

"My name is Sheik Tarik Oman," he said, taking a seat and fixing her with his intense dark gaze.

"Sheik..." She sat down as a shiver went up her spine. Wasn't that like a king in some countries? Was she in the presence of royalty? So that's why he thought everyone should drop what they were doing and cater to him.

"It's just a title. It means nothing...in this country," he explained.

She wanted to ask then why he expected special treatment from her? Being a sheik might mean nothing in this country, but she had a feeling it meant something somewhere else. Where people jumped when he told them to and obeyed his every wish. That happened in America too, only they didn't call such men sheiks, they called them dictatorial alpha males and Carolyn had had enough of them to last a lifetime. It was not only his title that gave away the sheik's royal standing, it was the way he carried himself—his shoulders back, his spine like a ramrod, his firm jaw jutting forward.

She sat down. "What can I do for you?" she asked, resigned to the fact that he'd taken over her time and her attention. She ought to order him out of the shop, but her clients had disappeared. She sighed. Once again she'd failed to assert her authority, even after her assertiveness training seminar. She shifted uncomfortably under his perusal, wishing for some unknown reason she'd had time to comb her unruly curls and apply some fresh makeup. After working nonstop since morning, she was sure she looked as haggard as she felt.

"You're a wedding planner," he said. "I want you to plan a wedding."

She automatically pulled out a form and attached it to her clipboard, intending to transfer the information to her computer later as she always did.

"First let me tell you my philosophy of wedding planning," she said. "Just to be sure we're both on the same page, so to speak."

"It's really not important what page you're on, Ms. Evans," the sheik said brusquely. "We'll begin on page one. You may have your own philosophy, I happen to have one of my own. Since I'm in charge of this wedding, we'll follow mine."

She blinked. No one had ever dismissed her philosophy so completely before they'd even heard it. They may have tuned out as she articulated it, but at least they were polite enough to let her expound for a few minutes. It didn't take that long. Life was too short to deal with this kind of man more than once in a lifetime. It wasn't too late to show the sheik to the door before they wasted any more of each other's time. And with this kind of a beginning, she already had a feeling they weren't going to get along. With this kind of groom, she felt sorry for the bride. Destined for a lifetime of being overruled and browbeaten. She'd been the observer of such a marriage for most of her life.

Carolyn took a deep breath. "What about the bride? Perhaps we should hear what she has to say."

"The bride is away at school. I'm paying for the wedding. I'm planning the wedding. Or I have been until now. Now I need help. Professional help. Your help. I'm not too proud to admit it." The way he said it sounded like admitting he needed help was something out of the ordinary for him. And that pride was his middle name. "I hear you're the best in the business," he added.

No use protesting. No use pretending she wasn't good at what she did. She might be the best but she sure wasn't the most successful or the richest. The rent on the shop had just been raised. So much so that she wondered if she and her partner could afford to stay in this prime location. Cash flow was sometimes iffy when clients were late or delinquent in paying. Which made her even more upset to think that this man had chased away her clients, maybe for good. However, one could certainly count on a sheik not to back out on his financial commitments, couldn't one?

She studied his darkly handsome face and his regal bearing from across the table and thought of all the reasons why she should turn him down immediately, before they went any further. One, he was domineering. Two, he was planning this wedding without the bride, always a recipe for trouble. Of course one-sided weddings were not that uncommon. Most brides took the initiative and made most of the plans. Choosing flowers and dresses were hardly something most men enjoyed doing. The participation of grooms at all was a recent phenomenon.

But a man coming in to plan his wedding without the bride was very unusual indeed. So much so she wondered why, how, what and who was the woman who'd snagged the gorgeous sheik and was willing to put up with his autocratic "I'm in charge here" ways. But she didn't ask that.

Instead she asked, "When do you plan to have this wedding, Mr...that is, your excellency, I mean..."

"In one month."

Carolyn gasped. "Planning a wedding in one month is impossible," she said firmly. "I have other clients, other commitments."

"Nothing is impossible. Difficult, yes. Impossible, no. Anyone in business knows that. There's always a way."

Carolyn pressed her lips together to keep from blurting something she'd regret, like go find another wedding consultant. One who doesn't mind taking orders from a dictator.

Oblivious to her dislike of his manner, he continued in the same vein. "I'm here because this wedding is very important to me. To me and my whole family. They're counting on *me* and I'm counting on *you.*" The intensity of his gaze made her knees knock together under the desk. Was that how he looked at his fiancée, too? Like he was going to eat her alive?

She had the feeling he was not going to take no for an answer. She had a feeling he *never* took no for an answer. And she was too tired to stay here and argue much longer.

Maybe it was just a small family affair to be held at home, which wouldn't require much work on her part. The least she could do was ask.

Carolyn held her clipboard between her and the sheik as if to ward off the vibrations emanating from the man who must be accustomed to giving orders and having them followed.

"Before I make a decision, I'll need to know some of the details. Now," she said, filling in the first blank on the form. "We have the date. What about the place?"

"Grace Cathedral."

She blinked. "Grace Cathedral?" The most sought-after site in the city for the weddings of the rich and famous. A gothic landmark that sat high above the city on Nob Hill.

"Yes, why not?" he said. "My sister is a convert to Christianity and her fiancé is a Protestant. So I made a sizable donation to the missionary fund and booked it some time ago as soon as we set a date. It seemed like a suitable and convenient location with enough room inside for both families as well as business associates. But that's as far as I've gotten. The rest is up to you."

"I see," she said, picturing the sheik waiting at the altar of the cathedral in his ceremonial headdress, the light shining through the stained glass windows on the bride as she came down the aisle. Carolyn had never done a wedding there but had always wanted to. She could almost smell the fragrant stephanotis she'd place at the end of each aisle, and hear the organ filling the magnificent church with music she'd help choose. She knew it could be the most spectacular, romantic wedding of the year if not the decade. And she'd be the one who planned it. The publicity wouldn't hurt business. Not at all.

Just as a matter of form, she went on to ask about flowers, ceremony, reception, officiant, photography, food, but he shrugged after each question saying he'd leave that to her and that money was no object. She realized that if she took this job she'd certainly be able to put her own stamp on this wedding.

To her surprise, Tarik stood up as if the interview was over, the decisions made and the contract signed. He held out his hand to shake hers. Probably the way they sealed the bargain in his culture. In her culture things weren't quite that simple. In fact, she didn't remember saying she would take the job.

"Just a minute," she said. "A handshake is not quite enough. I'll need you to sign this contract."

He shrugged, sat down again and signed the form she held out.

"One more thing," she said, suddenly overwhelmed by the thought of pulling off a large wedding in a month. "I'll need help. I can't do this by myself."

"Of course you can't," he said. "Where are your assistants? Surely you don't run an operation like this by yourself."

"I have a partner, but she's as busy as I am. We share the office and use the same florists and caterers and so on, but we each have our own clients. Both our calendars are filled up for the next year. When I say help I mean from you or from the bride. You need to at least be in on the decision making or you're going to be stuck with a wedding that doesn't reflect your lifestyle or your personality and you won't be happy. You want this to be a day you'll remember for the rest of your life."

"I'm sure I will," he said. "In every way possible. All right. You want some help. You want my input. You can have it. I can't stay any longer tonight, but if you come by tomorrow morning I'll meet with you before breakfast for one hour because that's how important this wedding is to me.'' He pounded his fist on the table for emphasis.

''That's very considerate,'' she said hoping she wasn't laying on the sarcasm too heavily. ''Some men don't devote even that much time to wedding planning. They leave it to the bride.''

''Perhaps they don't have as much at stake as I do,'' he said.

''Perhaps not. The bride must be a very special person,'' Carolyn said.

''Special, yes. But stubborn and headstrong, too. My sister is also a bit spoiled.''

Carolyn frowned. ''Your sister?''

''My sister Yasmine, the bride who is getting married in one month. I thought I made that clear. That is why I'm here. To hire you to plan her wedding.''

Carolyn stared at him. ''I see.'' But she didn't see, not really. What kind of a woman would trust her brother to plan her wedding? She told herself it didn't matter. She'd agreed to plan it and it was immaterial who the participants were. In one month it would be over, and she'd never hear of or see the sheik again. Something to look forward to.

''She's away at school in Switzerland,'' he explained. ''She has exams coming up so she won't be here until shortly before the wedding. When she arrives, everything will be in place—her dress, her flowers. Everything will go like clockwork.''

''It may go like clockwork. But on the other hand, most brides like to choose their own dress at least. And try it on. They must have wedding dresses in Switzerland. Perhaps she could buy one there.''

"She doesn't have time. And it won't be necessary," he said. "Stand up."

"What?"

"If I'm not mistaken, you are approximately the same size as my sister, which will eliminate the need for her to choose the dress and try it on. Stand up so I can be sure."

Reluctantly she got to her feet. His gaze was cool and appraising but he made her feel uncomfortably warm inside while goose bumps popped out on her skin. Couldn't he have simply asked her what size she was? Or didn't he know his sister's size to compare it with?

"Yes," he said, his eyes traveling slowly from the top of her head to the tips of her shoes, and lingering here and there as if he had all the time in the world. "I was right. You'll do."

Do? she wanted to ask. I'll *do?* Seething under her calm exterior, Carolyn sat down again.

"About my schedule," she said, her face still flushed from his lengthy scrutiny. "I don't know what kind of business you're in, but..."

"Oil."

Arab sheik. Oil. It figured. "Yes, well, in the bridal business we have weddings planned months or even years in advance. I can't just drop everything and concentrate on yours."

"I'm sure you'll be able to handle everything," he said smoothly. "Bearing in mind that my funds are unlimited, and this is a very important event."

"That's the way everyone feels about a wedding in the family. I'll do what I can but I hope you'll understand that I can't work full-time on this wedding. As it happens I *am* free tomorrow morning, shall we say nine?"

"Eight is better. Here's my address," he said handing

her a business card. "You see, there's always a way." There was so much certainty in his voice that she'd be there, that she wouldn't back out. Carolyn began to believe the sheik always got his way. She realized now how unlikely it was that the sheik himself would be getting married. What kind of a woman would marry him? Someone after his money, no doubt. No amount of money could tempt her to marry a man who called all the shots. Who micromanaged his wife's life. Even if he looked like a Hollywood version of a sheik with his exotic dark good looks and his royal bearing.

She couldn't help but pity his sister who would arrive at the last minute to put on her dress, chosen by him with the help of a paid consultant, walk down the aisle of a church selected by him, accompanied by music, ditto, ditto and so forth and so on. But who was she to object to her clients' strange ways. She was there to help them realize their dreams, even though she doubted the sheik had any dreams at all, just plans and goals and royal imperatives.

If he thought he was going to get away with one brief early morning meeting and then bow out and disappear until the wedding day, he was mistaken. As she said, if he didn't give her any input, he wasn't going to be happy with his sister's wedding. And if he wasn't happy with the way the wedding turned out, she had a feeling she'd hear about it. Loudly.

After she'd confirmed the appointment for the next day at his house—actually it was more of a command performance than an appointment—Carolyn set her clipboard down and stood. She felt like she'd just gone about ten rounds in the ring while avoiding being knocked out by a man who'd overwhelmed her with his attitude only to have the match declared a draw. She knew she was lucky she wasn't lying flat on her face while he held up his hand in a victory sign. Had he really won or had she? All she cared about at that moment was that it was over, at least for today. Tomorrow she'd be in better shape to cope with this man. To make it clear how decisions would be made.

"Closing up, going home?" he asked.

"Yes."

"It's late. I'll walk you to your car."

"That's not necessary. It's right in back of the shop."

"In back? It sounds dark and dangerous," he said. "I'm certain your husband wouldn't want you out there by yourself at this time of night."

"I always park there, and I've never been attacked yet," she said. "And I have no husband." Now why did she feel obliged to tell him that? It was none of his business. "I assure you I'll be fine. Furthermore I'm concerned your wife will be wondering why you're out so late." There, that served him right for the husband remark.

A brief flicker of amusement crossed his face as he glanced at his Rolex watch. "It's not that late," he said. "And if I had a wife, which I don't, I would still insist on walking you to your car. Any wife of mine would not expect me until she saw me."

"Her role would be taking care of the house, I suppose. Keeping your dinner warm and bringing you your pipe and slippers." She tried to keep her tone light, but a hint of bitterness crept into her voice at the memories of her mother doing just that. Submerging her own interests, her own life, year after year.

"That sounds appealing. But difficult to find someone like that in this day and age," he said.

"Which is why you aren't married, I imagine." She didn't know why she was engaging in this pointless banter with the sheik. It was really senseless to argue with him and though his accompanying her to her car was a trivial matter, she feared it was a bad omen for their future collaboration. Somehow she had to break the pattern of his giving orders and her giving in.

She'd never been able to assert herself while growing up in a house with an egomaniac, but she was grown-up now and in charge of her own life and her own business. She'd excommunicated her father from her life, and she'd learned to stand up for herself and what she believed. Of course putting what she'd learned into practice was another matter. To make things easier, she made it a point never to date a man with a strong will.

Actually she seldom dated at all these days since most of the men she met were on their way to the altar with someone else. She told herself that some day a kind, gentle, caring man who was not otherwise engaged would show up. They'd fall in love and then she'd be glad she'd saved herself for marriage and had never engaged in casual sex like some of her friends had. But with her thirtieth birthday on the horizon, she sometimes wondered when and if it would happen.

Normally she would have taken the time to clear up the loose ends on her desk, check her e-mail and enter the data. But with the sheik standing there watching her every move like a hawk, all she could manage at that point was to grab her jacket, turn off the lights and lock the front door. She felt his hand on her elbow as they walked out the back exit, guiding her firmly as if she was some kind of fragile flower who might stumble without his help. As if she couldn't manage to get to her car by herself, which she'd been doing safely for the past eight years. And if that weren't enough macho male chauvinism for one night, he took her keys from her hand and unlocked her car door for her. She told herself he was from a different country, a different culture, where men were men and women stayed behind tall walls and heavy veils.

"Thank you," she said stiffly.

"Until tomorrow," he said, lowering his head in a slight bow.

She nodded and drove away at full speed, though what she was trying to escape she didn't know. He was only a client, a man who'd hired her to manage his sister's wedding. In her rearview mirror she saw him standing there in the alleyway while the rain bounced off his impeccable suit, a tall, dark mysterious figure watching her until she was out of sight. She turned her car heater up to high to combat the chills that suddenly attacked her. But nothing helped. She was still shaking when she got home. Due to a stranger who walked into her life tonight. Tomorrow, things would be different. Even though she'd be on his turf, she'd show him she was in charge. He might control a whole oil company, but he didn't control her.

Chapter Two

The next morning she drove to his house at the end of a tree-lined street in the prestigious and aptly named area of San Francisco called Sherwood Forest. It was a long, low house on at least an acre of prime real estate overlooking the Pacific Ocean. After driving through the open gate and parking her compact car in the circular driveway, she gave a quick check in the visor mirror, pleased to see the circles under her eyes had disappeared thanks to the cucumber slices she'd placed on them for twenty minutes this morning. A necessity because she'd spent entirely too much time lying in bed the night before tossing and turning and replaying her conversation with the sheik. And wishing she'd said no to him.

The whole situation was too bizarre. It was not just the situation, it was him. As sleep eluded her she couldn't shake the image of the dark ebony hair that matched his dark eyes that seemed to bore right through her, or the sound of his slightly accented deep voice. If someone had to plan the sister's wedding, why couldn't it be their father? If he was around, wouldn't he be a more appropriate person to plan the wedding? She could have dealt better with an old, fatherly sheik who didn't exude such masculine virility. Who didn't make her feel so aware of his overpowering presence.

Sooner or later they were going to come to blows. Not real blows of course, but verbal ones, and Carolyn was not going to give in. Not if she knew she was right. She had the right to conduct her business the way she saw fit and if he didn't like it, he could find someone else. If she'd learned anything after leaving home at eighteen, it was to stand firm on her principles. Confronting the sheik would be the ultimate test. They didn't come any more macho or determined than he did.

By morning Carolyn had come to her senses, realized that the sheik was just a man, a little more virile than most, but certainly nothing she couldn't handle. And more importantly, his sister's wedding was an opportunity she couldn't pass up. This job would be a lot of work, yes, but it would be over in one month. It was a chance to do a spectacular, dream wedding in a beautiful cathedral, which just might give her career the boost it needed. It could lead to other big weddings, ones where they gave her decent notice, like a year in advance. Yes, this was short notice, but with her energy and organizational skills, she ought to be able to pull it off. She had to try. And the first order of business was to find out if the invitations had been sent. She should have asked last night, but her mind seemed to have taken a leave of absence at the time.

At the massive front door, she knocked and pressed the bell. A tall, dark-skinned woman in a graceful silk sari answered the door and looked her up and down for a long moment without speaking a word.

"Carolyn Evans.... I'm here to see Mr. Tarik Oman, I mean the sheik, that is."

"Ah, yes. The wedding consultant." The woman spoke in heavily accented English "Will you come into the library?"

Before she entered the library, Carolyn gaped at the formal living room and the majestic staircase leading to the second floor. She hoped she'd get a tour of the place sooner or later. Instead of going off to fetch the sheik, the woman closed the door behind her and stood with her back to the floor-to-ceiling shelves of leather-bound books.

"I just wonder," the woman asked, "if you know what you're doing."

"Oh yes, I've planned many weddings. I'm looking forward to working on this one. I'm sure it will turn out fine."

"It's wrong. All wrong. It won't work."

"Don't worry," Carolyn assured her. "Of course it's short notice, but I'm sure it will work. It will all come together. Believe me, it always does." Prewedding jitters were nothing new to her, but who was this woman and what was her role in the wedding? Carolyn had started the day with high hopes, planning to get off to a good start with this project, but the first person she'd run into was already voicing her doubts. She had a fleeting thought of her office where she would have been if it hadn't been for the sheik, sipping coffee while she looked through the phone book for a harpist for a garden wedding in May. It was the sheik's idea to have her come at eight. If she'd known he was going to keep her waiting she would have insisted he come to her office.

There was a long silence while the woman closed her

eyes and pressed her hand to her forehead. Carolyn didn't know if she had gone into a trance, was worried about the wedding or just tired. She cleared her throat, and the woman turned abruptly and opened the door.

"Very well," the woman said. "I'm going to make tea. You'll find *him* in the pool room." She waved her hand toward a sliding glass door.

Carolyn stepped lightly across the vast Oriental carpet in the great room and opened the door. There was no doubt who him was. But why was he playing pool at this hour of the morning? Didn't sheiks have anything better to do? Like manage their oil business? At the end of the hall she found herself in a huge glass-enclosed solarium with a retractable roof above an impressive mosaic-tiled swimming pool.

She stopped dead in her tracks at the even more impressive sight of the man who emerged from the pool, his broad shoulders covered with droplets of water, his tanned chest covered with fine swirls of dark hair and the rest of him barely covered at all with a European swimsuit. Oh, my. She felt her cheeks flush. Maybe she was wrong. Maybe she couldn't deal with all this testosterone, at least not this early in the morning.

She jerked her gaze from his lower body and forced herself to look him in the eye as he approached her. She thought she'd prepared herself to see the man today, but nothing could have prepared her for the sight of a partially clad gorgeous man. Why couldn't he have met her in the library, preferably fully-clothed.

"Hello," he said, draping a towel around his shoulders. "Forgive me for greeting you so informally. I didn't know you were here, or I would have met you elsewhere. Appropriately dressed. How did you get in? Where is Meera?'' he asked with a frown.

''A tall woman wearing a sari and a disapproving look?''

''I'm afraid she's angry with me,'' he said. ''She lets me know it by neglecting her duties. What can I say? She's been with our family for two generations. She's old and set in her ways. I'd be lost without her, and she without me, but sometimes...''

''She's making tea,'' Carolyn noted.

''Good. That's one thing I can rely on her for. A decent tea. I shall meet you in the library.''

She looked at her watch.

''I know, you're a busy woman. We'll begin our work shortly,'' he said. ''Do you swim?''

''Not at eight in the morning,'' she said. Although at that moment, she could think of nothing more appealing than to plunge her whole overheated, overstimulated body into a pool of cool water.

''I see,'' he said, his gaze once again—for the second time in twenty-four hours—traveling the length of her body, lingering on her hips and moving to her breasts as if he could see right through her suit to her silk, pale lavender underwear. But this time his appraisal was not as cool as the one in her office last night. In fact his gaze was downright heated this morning. Causing a shiver to move up her spine. And a slight weakness in the knees. Ridiculous. The look in his eyes could have nothing to do with her. It was just his way. After all, she was an underling he'd hired. He was a sheik. He said he didn't have a wife, but maybe he had a harem. Maybe he was sizing her up as a future member. The idea ought to have had her running for her life. Instead she stood there, rooted to the spot.

Whether his gaze was personal or not, she wondered

somewhere in the back of her mind whether he approved of what he saw. She'd taken care to choose a tailored suit, business-like, but fitted as if it had been made for her. Her partner, Lily, said it was her Ally McBeal suit with the skirt substantially above the knees. So she wasn't as thin as the TV lawyer, or as muscular as a fitness center model, but no one had ever accused her of being overweight or out of shape.

"And now, if you'll excuse me for a moment. I'll get dressed," he said.

She'd only been there for fifteen minutes and already she was breathing hard as she walked back to the library, seething with frustration. When was this so-called eight o'clock meeting going to take place? This wasn't a job, it was a way of life, and she had her own way of life, thank you very much. One which she was extremely anxious to get back to. To the safety of her shop where *she* was in charge.

Tarik toweled off quickly and dressed, choosing a pair of charcoal gray slacks and a white Egyptian cotton shirt. Everyone he'd spoken to said Carolyn Evans was the best wedding consultant in town, but no one had mentioned she had masses of auburn curls and eyes the intriguing color of the Arabian Gulf during a storm.

No one had told him whether she was married or not either. Why should they? It had nothing to do with her competence. Then why had he troubled himself to find out? Simple curiosity? Or did it have something to do with her alluring body or exquisite legs that went on forever? He knew these were not relevant qualifications for a bridal consultant, still...she'd caught him off guard. He smiled to himself as he remembered her checking his marital status as well.

Frankly, he'd expected someone older, plainer, with glasses and sensible shoes instead of high heels and a snug-fitting suit that hugged her curves in a most captivating way. When he saw her, he actually hoped she had a husband and was off limits. Husband or not, he reminded himself sternly, she was still off limits to him.

Seeing her through the window of her shop last night, he almost turned away, not wishing to be distracted by an attractive woman at this crucial time. Especially an independent American woman. He'd had experience with women of that type when he'd first arrived in this country. With one in particular. He'd been overwhelmed by her vitality, her dazzling good looks and her freedom to make her own choices. So overwhelmed he'd fallen head over heels in love. Or so he'd thought.

When his father learned of his involvement with the woman, he made it clear he was not pleased with Tarik's choice. He warned that marriages of the heart were not advisable for the heir to such wealth and power. Witness his own happy marriage to Tarik's mother, which had been arranged by their parents. His father offered to broker a marriage with a suitable girl, the daughter of his best friend. Blinded by infatuation, and offended by his father's interference, Tarik refused. His father angrily reprimanded him and reminded him of his duty to his family, but Tarik wouldn't listen. Later, he wished he had.

There was no need at this point to tell Ms. Evans there was more to this wedding than the joining of two people in matrimony. He would tell her all she needed to know to plan the wedding. Nothing more, nothing less. If he told her the whole story, she might object, and he didn't want to hear any more objections from the women in his life who didn't understand his position.

He was relieved to see that Meera, however angry she was about the nuptials, had at least provided a tray of mint tea and small cookies and lighted a fire in the fireplace chasing the chill from the early morning air. Carolyn Evans was studying a portrait on the wall.

"My father," he explained, handing her a cup of tea. When his hand brushed hers he felt a slight jolt of electricity. Obviously the combination of dry air and the thick, hand-knotted carpet. She gave him a quick glance, but otherwise she appeared not to notice anything unusual had occurred.

"I see the resemblance," she said looking at the painting.

"Thank you. I only hope I can live up to his reputation. He was an astute businessman and a wise leader."

She took a seat on a leather couch and crossed her legs. He had to drag his gaze back to hers. He must not ogle the wedding consultant's long legs. Especially not on day one when he only had a short time to spend with her. This was business, after all. He had no time for pleasure.

"Will your father be here for the wedding?" she asked.

"In spirit only," Tarik said. "He died two years ago."

"I'm sorry," she said softly. He was surprised to hear there was real sympathy in her voice and in her eyes. After all, she barely knew him.

"Are your parents alive?" he asked.

"My mother is, my father is too, actually, but he's not a part of my life."

He raised his eyebrows. A father not a part of his child's life? He wanted to ask why not. But he could tell by the shuttered look in her eyes she wasn't eager to talk about it. In his world, no matter how old the child, the parents must be respected. It had been a hard lesson but he'd learned it well. Thank goodness he'd learned it before it was too late to reconcile with his father.

"I feel my father's spirit guiding me in business and family matters every day, especially with this wedding. I believe he would be pleased to know you are helping me achieve my goal to honor his memory."

"I hope so," she murmured, gazing at him over her teacup with her extraordinary gray-green eyes. It must be the morning light from the windows on the east that made them so luminous.

He set his cup on the table and sat on a low ottoman facing her, his legs stretched out in front of him, tenting his fingers together thoughtfully, unable to tear his gaze from hers. If he did tell her everything, would she join forces with the other women in his life and go against him? Or would she understand his point of view and help him bring about the solution to all his problems? Whether she understood or not, she had to help him. She'd agreed to do that. That was her job. That's what he was paying her for. Heaven knew he needed an ally at this time but this was not the time to confide in a stranger. No matter that she was a beautiful stranger at that. The only thing he wanted from her was to have the wedding go off without a hitch.

"In my culture there is nothing more important than family," he added. "Fulfilling my father's goals and unfinished business has become my highest priority."

Carolyn nodded. As if she understood. It was the way she was looking at him, so intently, her gaze unwavering. He felt hope rising somewhere deep inside, hope that if she did know what was going on behind the scenes she would not launch into a discussion about the importance of love and romance and other female illusions.

"The unfinished business has to do with oil?" she asked.

"Just so," he said. For a long moment neither one spoke. The library was his favorite room, made for quiet contemplation, but today the only thing he could contemplate was Carolyn Evans. He knew it was wrong. He knew she was off limits, that she was a passing attraction, but he wondered if she felt it, too. Never mind if she did. It would lead to nothing. The reason he couldn't take his eyes off of her, the reason he'd dreamed of her last night was just because he was overworked with the upcoming merger of his oil company and the largest privately held refinery in the U.S. She was a distraction, and he couldn't afford any distractions now. Not with the wedding and the merger so close at hand.

Finally Carolyn broke the silence. "I assume you and your sister are very close," she said at last. "Or she wouldn't allow you to plan her wedding for her."

"We've had our differences," he admitted. "Since my father died I became head of the family and her guardian. At first she had a hard time accepting that fact. Perhaps she still does. She's young and has a strong will. They say it runs in the family," he said with a wry smile. "Nonetheless, we agree on most things. Divorce is not an option in our culture. Not the way it is in America where people marry for romantic love then get divorced when they find the thrills don't last."

"Sometimes divorce is the only way out of a bad situation," Carolyn said, her eyes fixed on the tea leaves in the bottom of her cup. "But I'd like to believe that true love can last forever."

"Are you speaking from personal experience?" he asked. "Have you ever been married or divorced?" Or in love? he wanted to ask. But it was none of his business, and it was not an appropriate question to ask a stranger.

"Neither," she said. "I've never been married." She hesitated for a long moment. "I don't believe in divorce either. Not for frivolous reasons. But sometimes there is no other way."

"You speak of true love," he said. "By that I can only hope you mean respect and admiration and not an emotional attachment. Because a marriage based on emotion doesn't stand a chance of surviving. If women ever feel the way they're supposed to feel when they fall in love—that they've been struck by lightning, the pulse speeds up, the knees are weak and the heart pounds—they probably should be taken immediately to the emergency room. They're either having a heart attack or a stroke. Men, on the other hand, are level-headed and sensible and are not susceptible to such phenomena. They marry for practical purposes. To ensure offspring to continue the lineage or for companionship."

She gave him a brief smile that was over too soon. He knew she didn't believe him. He wished he could say something to make her really smile. To see those lips curve upward and her beautiful eyes light up.

"Then you don't believe in romantic love," she said.

"Ah, now you understand," he said. "Love is an exaggerated notion put forth by poets and songwriters. I can understand instant attraction, if that's what you're talking about. A chemical reaction that sometimes happens between two people that produces some of the effects I mentioned. But these feelings don't last." It was a pity they didn't. But there it was.

"Well," she said, opening her briefcase. "Shall we get down to work? I've brought some pictures of some possible locations for the reception."

She spread the photographs on the large dark walnut library table and they stood side by side while she told him the benefits of the Octagon House versus the advantages of the historic gardens at Filoli or the wild Marin headlands.

To be honest, and he was always scrupulously honest with himself, Tarik found himself more aware of the woman next to him than the pictures of the reception sites. It was partly the subtle scent she wore of wild roses that made him want to get closer to her, to inhale deeply and let it permeate his senses. It was partly the way her hair brushed against her cheek that made him want to wrap the curls around his fingers. Finally he had to move away. To clear his head. To reaffirm his purpose.

"What is it?" she asked. "What's wrong? Don't you like them?"

"I like them fine," he said brusquely from the other side of the table. But did he? Did he even know what he'd seen? He began to wish he'd insisted she do this wedding completely by herself. Or that he'd kept looking until he found the other kind of wedding consultant. The older one with thick ankles, a no-nonsense air and iron-gray hair.

Fortunately this meeting would be over soon, and he'd make it clear she was on her own. He'd send her on her way with a few suggestions and let her do the work. That's what he was paying her for. He didn't want to spend anymore time than necessary with her. She disturbed him with her manner, both competent and calm, and her looks, both sexy and subdued. He didn't want to think about her the way he had last night after he left her office. Remembering the color of her eyes and the rose tint of her complexion. Which led to those disturbing dreams of her he'd had. He had to keep his mind on important matters of money, merger and family honor. Both day and night.

He started to usher her out of the house before she could

disturb him anymore today, but before she left she paused in front of a small oil painting of the white-walled family compound on the Gulf of Arabia.

"How beautiful," she murmured.

"Even more beautiful in actuality," he said. "It is where I grew up. The property has been in the family for generations. And now it is mine."

She nodded and finally she left. He breathed a sigh of relief, wishing that her subtle scent did not linger in the library the way it did.

Chapter Three

As Carolyn walked to her car she had the distinct feeling she'd been hustled out of the house abruptly for some unknown reason before they'd barely finished talking through the wedding plans. Even when she lingered to admire the painting, she sensed his restlessness. Was he afraid she'd never leave? Was he suddenly sorry he'd hired her? Had she said the wrong thing? She went over the conversation in her mind. Of their talk about love and marriage. She didn't want to get involved in a personal discussion with the man. But somehow she had.

However personal it had been, however much he'd learned about her, and she'd learned about his family, she still didn't know if he himself had ever been involved with a woman. Or why he was planning his sister's wedding by himself. His explanations just didn't hold water. There wasn't a woman alive who wouldn't stop everything, even in the middle of finals, to at least buy herself a wedding dress. If she was as excited about the wedding as she should be. If she was as much in love with the groom as she should be, that is.

The groom. No one had mentioned him. Who was he? She didn't even know his name. Carolyn had forgotten to ask the most basic questions. The groom's family might want some say in these proceedings. At the very least, she ought to meet them and put them in the loop.

And what about the invitations? Again, she'd forgotten all about them. What was wrong with her? This man had the ability to make her forget everything. Including a list of questions she'd prepared for him. She got out of her car and walked back up to the front door. Before she even knocked Tarik opened the door. As if he expected her. As if he was waiting for her. But he didn't look particularly happy to see her again from the way his eyebrows were drawn together in a frown.

"I...uh...I forgot to ask you if you've sent the invitations."

"That's your job," he said.

"Then I ought to know what name to put on them. You've never mentioned the groom. Who is he?"

"Jeffrey Branson."

Branson. The Bransons were an old prominent San Francisco family. They had made their original fortune from silver mines in the last century. Now they were involved in...what? Refineries, railroads, lumber?

"Do you know him?" Tarik asked.

"No." As if she hobnobbed with high society. "But I've heard of the family of course. What does Jeffrey do?"

"He's involved in the family business."

"Which is what exactly?"

"An independent oil refinery."

"Oil," she said. "Like your family."

"Not exactly. We produce crude oil, the Bransons are in the business of refining and distributing it."

"You must have a lot in common. It sounds like a match made in heaven," Carolyn said.

Tarik nodded. "My feelings exactly."

The way he said it, with a slight emphasis on *my* gave Carolyn a moment's pause. Was this a match made in heaven or somewhere else?

"I gather you like Jeffrey."

Tarik's expression hardened, and she knew right away she'd overstepped some imaginary boundary and intruded into his personal life. "Whether I like him is beside the point and really none of your business. He's a suitable match for my sister, that is what counts."

Carolyn had an overwhelming desire to up and quit right then and there. The man was insufferable. *Suitable match. None of your business.* Of course it was her business to know as much as possible about the bride and groom and the two families involved. But she'd learned that losing her temper in the face of male dogmatism was pointless. Instead she took a deep breath.

"You're right," she said as calmly as possible. "If your sister loves him, that's all that matters."

If she thought that was the tactful thing to say, she was wrong. If she thought that would end the discussion, she didn't know the sheik. Tarik looked like a black cloud had passed overhead. He positively glowered at her.

"I thought," he said, bracing his hands on the solid door frame, "that I'd made it clear how I felt about marrying for love. It's a poor excuse for respect and admiration and duty."

"Yes, you said that, but..."

"But you persist in believing that the decision of a lifetime be made on the feelings of a nineteen-year-old girl and her fiancé. Fortunately I know better. As I said before, it doesn't matter how you feel, Ms. Evans. Your job is to plan the wedding. I remember distinctly your complaining to me about the lack of notice I've given you to come up with this wedding, thus I advise you to not waste your time discussing these trivial, frivolous matters with me when we both have better things to do."

Carolyn swallowed hard. He was dismissing her in no uncertain terms, dismissing her legitimate concerns and questions as well. It was time to take a stand. She straightened her shoulders.

"May I remind you, Mr. Oman, that I have planned over seventy-five weddings in my career and you, to the best of my knowledge, have planned none at all. I would never presume to tell you how to run your oil business so I would hope you would allow me to do my job as I see fit. It doesn't matter to me who the participants in the wedding are. How they met or why or how they're getting married is not relevant.

"I have done a wedding for trapeze artists under the big top and a hot-air balloon wedding at two-hundred feet in the air and I've never questioned anyone's motives for getting married or their allegiance to each other. What is important to me and I hope to you, is that the wedding goes smoothly and that it meets the expectations of both the bride and groom's families, no matter who is paying. That's my job and I believe I've been reasonably successful at it. Or you wouldn't have sought me out and asked me to take the job. Would you?"

He stared at her as if she'd asked him to swallow a bitter pill.

"Fine," he said at last. But the tone of his voice told

her it wasn't fine at all. "Feel free to ask all the questions you'd like. But not now. I have a conference call in five minutes, and I believe we both need a break to think things over. You have your work cut out for you and so do I. I look forward to hearing from you regarding the reception."

"First things first. If you want to fill Grace Cathedral, the invitations must be ordered and sent out immediately. Who's announcing the marriage?"

"I am," he said. "I thought I'd made that clear."

"The bride's full name?"

"Yasmine Noor Oman."

Carolyn reached for a pencil and scribbled on a small notebook she retrieved from her purse. "I'll need a picture of her for the newspaper. I assume you'll want to put it in."

"Of course. And oh yes, don't forget about the honeymoon."

"What?" Carolyn gasped. Plan the honeymoon, too? What next? The christening of their first child?

"The honeymoon. Make the necessary reservations."

"But I can't possibly make that decision, not without..."

"I wonder, Ms Evans, how you've come so far in your chosen field with your negative attitude. Can't is a word I refuse to listen to in my business. I'd advise you to avoid using it. If you really can't make the decision, at least you can give me a list of options. Agreed?"

Back at the shop on Union Street, Carolyn couldn't remember if she'd actually agreed or simply marched away from the house, speechless with disbelief and indignation. She tossed her briefcase on her desk, threw herself into a chair and exhaled loudly, as if to expel all the frustrations she'd been holding back for the past few hours.

"Where have you been?" her partner Lily asked, looking up from a desk covered with papers.

"I've been to a sheik's palace," she said.

"A real, honest-to-God sheik?" Lily asked. She looked impressed, and it was hard to impress Lily. She'd been in the business longer than Carolyn. Seen every kind of wedding and every type of bride and groom. "Was it business...or pleasure?" she asked with a grin.

"Business of course," Carolyn said. "He came in last evening, interrupted a meeting I had about the Trenter wedding and insisted I drop everything and plan his wedding."

"Who is the sheik marrying?" Lily asked. "Not a commoner, I hope."

"No one. No one would marry him. When you meet him you'll understand why."

"Old? Ugly?" Lily asked.

Carolyn shook her head. "Young and handsome. But his personality! He makes my father look like Mr. Nice Guy."

"That bad?"

"Worse. He gives orders like you're his personal servant. Who I actually just met by the way. No, this is his sister's wedding, only he's doing all the planning. Or rather I am. I think."

"How come you didn't turn him down if he's so obnoxious?" Lily asked.

"For one thing it's a plum job, a big society wedding that could put I DO! I DO! on the map for sure. Bring in some good money, too."

"Nevertheless, I can't see you working with a tyrant, Carolyn. You have a problem with authority figures," Lily said.

"But I'm learning, aren't I? At least I thought I was. Until Sheik Tarik Oman walked in here last night. This is the kind of guy to try my patience, to test everything I've ever learned about assertiveness, anger management, you name it. The problem is working with him is likely to set me back a few years. I could end up in therapy for years. What do you think? Should I call and tell him I can't do it?''

She answered her own question. ''It's not worth it. Not for the money, not for the prestige. I didn't tell you but it's scheduled for one month from now, and he hasn't ordered the invitations. Fortunately he has reserved the church, but that's all. No, I can't do it.'' She reached for the phone.

''Sounds like a real challenge,'' Lily said mildly. ''If you can work with this guy, you can work with anybody.''

Carolyn set the phone down. ''You'd do it, wouldn't you? Do you want the job?''

Lily shook her head. ''I'm overwhelmed. Three weddings this month, four next. If I'd been here I would have turned him down flat. But then I didn't see him, did I? I'm just as susceptible to good-looking men as the next forty-three-year-old married lady. What did you say he looked like? Fill me in, I've never seen a sheik before. Does he wear one of those headdresses? Did he ride in on a camel? Does he have a wife?''

''No, no and no,'' Carolyn said, leaning back in her chair. ''I can't imagine anyone marrying him, except for his money. He's got dark hair and dark eyes, and he looks just like your average, everyday sheik.'' She shrugged nonchalantly as if his looks had made no particular impression on her, but they had. She couldn't shake the image of the man in his library, seated across from her, his dark gaze locked on hers, making her feel like she was melting on the inside. Couldn't forget the painting of the villa on the sea or the portrait of his father who looked so much like him, an older, kinder, gentler sheik. A hint of what the young man would or could become. If he mellowed with time. An interesting thought, but not very likely.

"Just an average, everyday sheik, hmmm?" Lily said, interrupting her reverie. "If he doesn't wear one of those white headdresses, what does he wear?"

"Oh, you know, just the usual..." The image of the sheik emerging from the swimming pool in nothing but his Speedo swimsuit barely concealing his masculine attributes caused the heat to flood Carolyn's cheeks, which was not lost on her astute partner.

"I've got to see this guy," Lily said with a smile. "When are you getting together next?"

"I don't know. Honestly, a few minutes ago I would have said never."

"Never say never," Lily cautioned. "You can do it. I know you can. It sounds like a great opportunity for you. Both professionally and personally. Everyone will ask who planned this spectacular event. You'll get your name in the paper, you'll pull in some money and you'll show yourself once and for all that you've got what it takes to stand up to a man with guts."

"Guts? That's putting it kindly." But Carolyn knew Lily was right as usual. Every time Carolyn had shied away from a difficult project, Lily had urged her on. She'd learned a lot from the older woman and her advice was usually right on. But then Lily hadn't seen the sheik.

So Carolyn swallowed her apprehensions and plunged ahead. After all, they had a signed contract. She spent the day on the phone to the printer, researching reception sites, caterers and even honeymoon locations for the sheik's sister. Since the sheik hadn't given her even a clue as to where his sister would like to go on her honeymoon, she decided to plan it as if it were her own. If they didn't like it, they could find their own destination.

As for her, she'd always wanted to go to a tropical island and stay in a thatched hut on a secluded beach that was rustic and luxurious at the same time. Where she and her new husband would make love for the first time under the stars. Where the sensual pleasures of lovemaking would unfold in endless ways on endless days. Where she would know that she was right to wait until her marriage to make love with the man of her dreams.

Who that man would be wasn't clear. Perhaps it would never happen. Maybe he didn't exist. But that didn't take away the vicarious pleasure of planning Yasmine Oman's honeymoon. At five o'clock she said goodbye to Lily and started out the door for an appointment. At the door she was met by his highness, Tarik Oman, looking more regal and handsome than that morning, if possible. If she had a half a brain she'd back out right now and tell him she couldn't possibly do this wedding. All he was doing was standing in the doorway and suddenly her palms were damp and her brain had turned to mush. She could barely remember where she was going. She clutched her briefcase to her side.

"I'm glad I caught you," he said. "I was in the neighborhood and I have some matters to discuss with you. I find face-to-face meetings are always more productive, don't you?" he asked.

"Yes, of course. But not now. I have an appointment...with the printer...now, in ten minutes. She's staying late to accommodate me, so if you'll excuse me...." She tried to edge past him, but he didn't move. Of course she could squeeze by, but if he didn't move it would mean coming into intimate contact with his body, pressing her breasts against his chest.

"Fine," he said, but he still didn't budge an inch. "I'll go along. We can talk along the way. My car is right here."

She was about to say she preferred to take her own car and go by herself because it was more efficient that way when the truth was she didn't want to spend anymore time with him than absolutely necessary, but on the other hand, she really needed him to see the invitations. While they were standing there at an impasse, sizing each other up, Lily got up from her desk and introduced herself.

Carolyn had almost forgotten she was there. That was the effect Tarik had on her. There was something about the man that disturbed her, caused temporary amnesia and attracted her like a magnet at the same time. Something that caused her voice to falter and her surroundings to fade away.

She waited anxiously for Tarik to display some of his arrogant, boorish behavior, just enough to convince Lily and herself that she hadn't exaggerated, but he took the opportunity to turn on his considerable royal charm. Carolyn could tell her partner was eating out of his hand and wouldn't believe a word of what Carolyn had told her. When she finally interrupted their conversation to say she was leaving immediately, she thought Tarik was going to kiss Lily's hand. And Lily would have let him. Honestly, the man was not to be believed.

Before she knew what was happening, Carolyn was ensconced in Tarik's foreign convertible and they were driving down Union Street, which was crowded with cars and pedestrians going to the upscale shops or heading for the many coffee bars in the trendy neighborhood.

She gave him directions to the printer and then crossed

her arms over her waist. "What do you want?" she asked, unable to stop the defensive tone in her voice. He put her on edge, that's what he did. Especially when she hadn't been expecting him, and had no time to prepare herself for the encounter. Now here she was sitting next to him in his expensive new car with a dozen controls in front of her for the sound system, the heater, the air-conditioning, navigation system and whatever else came with a car like that.

"To see you."

"Yes, I gathered that. What about?"

"About the wedding, of course," he spoke slowly as if speaking to a simpleton.

"I've been working on it all day but so far I have nothing definite to report," she said briskly. "Which I would have told you if you'd called first. It would have saved you a trip to my office. I've left messages here and there but I don't have anything definite yet. About the honeymoon..."

"What about it?"

"Can you at least tell me which continent they want to go to, or if they like the beach or the mountains or a big city? Do they do outdoor sports? I can't believe they haven't given you any information."

"Believe it," he said. "They're both busy people. Especially now. Which is why the responsibility has landed on me and by extension, on you. I assure you they'll be grateful to you for all you're doing. What is the customary destination for honeymoons in this country? Isn't it Niagara Falls?"

Carolyn stifled a smile. "Yes, that is a traditional honeymoon destination, or it was some seventy-five years ago."

"Out of date, I see. Well, then, if it were you, where would you want to go?"

"Oh, I don't know," she said nonchalantly as if she hadn't been dreaming about it for years. "Somewhere warm, I suppose," she said, leaning back in her seat as he drove down Geary Street toward the printer. She pictured that tropical island she'd dreamed of, warm sun and cool breezes and bare skin.

"An island, perhaps, like Hawaii?" he asked.

"Hawaii is too crowded, too civilized. I'd want to get away from phones and faxes and traffic. If it were me I'd choose one of those small islands in the South Pacific near Fiji where you can have a thatched hut and a private beach all to yourselves."

"I see. Warm weather so you can act uncivilized and throw away inhibitions, wear very few clothes and have the privacy to make love whenever you like, night or day. Yes, it sounds very appealing."

She felt his eyes on her. Heard the sensual innuendo in his voice and maybe even a trace of longing. Did the sheik have dreams, too? He said he didn't believe in romantic love, but he probably believed in sex. Most men did. She reached for one of the dashboard controls to get some air to cool her flushed cheeks. But she turned on the radio instead. Strains of a piano concerto came from the speakers. He covered her hand with his broad fingers and guided her fingers to adjust the air conditioning as if he knew what she wanted. Just the touch of his hand caused her heartbeat to speed up. As the cool air obediently shot out of a vent, she knotted her fingers in her lap and stared straight ahead. Why did his touch have such a disturbing effect on her? He was just another client, just another man.

"But you don't need to wait for your honeymoon to enjoy a romantic interlude," he said with a glance in her direction. "You Americans do such things without being married."

"I don't," she said firmly. "I intend to wait for my honeymoon."

"Really. Then you are a..."

"Yes," she said quickly before he could say the word that made her so nervous. She turned to look out the side window so he wouldn't see her blush. She didn't know why or how they'd gotten onto this subject. As if he cared. Besides it was a personal decision she didn't share with everyone. Or anyone for that matter. Here she was blurting out her most intimate secret to a client. Not even a friend. What possessed her to tell him?

"That's the printer on the corner," she said.

Actually it was good he'd come with her to proofread the invitations before they went to be engraved. After he'd made a few corrections and she'd made a few suggestions, they agreed on a final version:

Sheik Tarik Oman
requests the honor of your presence
at the wedding of his sister
Yasmine Noor
and
Mr. Jeffrey Philip Branson
at five o'clock in the evening
Saturday, the tenth of June
Grace Cathedral
San Francisco, California
Reception following
Please R.S.V.P.

"Uh-oh," Carolyn said staring at the blank space after Reception following. "We've got to get the reception nailed down right away. When are you sending these to be printed?'' she asked the woman who was helping them.

''They should go tomorrow. You haven't given us much time.''

Carolyn gave Tarik a look that conveyed the fact that it was his fault they had so little time to plan the wedding and not hers.

''Then we'll find a place for the reception tonight,'' Tarik said. ''And let you know in the morning.'' He gave the woman a brief smile and with his hand under Carolyn's elbow, guided her out the door.

She ground her back teeth together. She didn't need help walking from the shop to the car. What did he think, she was going to fall off the curb?

''You don't know what you're saying,'' she said, standing next to his car. ''This is not how it's done. You don't just go out and find a place for a reception. You look at the list of possible places, study the brochures, which you didn't seem interested in doing this morning, then you make calls, then...''

He opened the car door. ''That's your way. Mine is to take action. What about the top floor penthouse of one of the famous hotels? Someplace with a view.''

''That would be fine,'' she said, ''but I'm sure they're already booked for months ahead.''

''Get in,'' he said.

His first stop was the famous Mark Hopkins Hotel. When they approached the office of the events director, and they heard the woman say just what Carolyn thought she'd say—they had been booked solid for years—she couldn't help feeling smug that she was right and he was wrong. But Tarik didn't seem discouraged. He simply took her hand and they hurried across the street to the Fairmont Hotel. She didn't want to hold his hand. The less physical contact with him the better.

On the other hand, dashing across California Street with him was an exhilarating experience. With the wind in her hair and the solid warmth of his hand in hers, she felt protected and daring at the same time. What was it about him that made an ordinary street crossing exciting? It was because he wasn't ordinary. Far from it. He was a sheik. He came from a long line of generations of camel-riding, oil-rich sheiks before him. He was raised to assume responsibility, to take care of his family. He was raised to give orders, to have servants and maybe even a harem.

If anyone had asked her yesterday if she would be interested in meeting a sheik, or if she thought sheiks were romantic, she would have responded with an overwhelming no. Today she couldn't be quite so negative. Today she was standing on top of Nob Hill, unwillingly holding hands with a sheik, looking out over San Francisco Bay at dusk. From the looks of him he could be anybody. No royal headdress, no flowing robes, no royal steed in sight. *Yes, he could be anybody,* she thought, a cursory glance in his direction. Anybody who was breathtakingly handsome, dressed with impeccable taste, had his clothes tailored just for him and who exuded confidence. The lights of the Bay Bridge went on as they watched, as if just for them, and the whole scene was transformed into a fairyland. As if he was the prince and she was the princess in the glass slipper.

"It's a beautiful city," he said as if they had nothing better to do but to stand there and enjoy the view.

"Will you stay here in San Francisco?" she asked. "Or return to your country some day."

"It looks more and more as if I'll be staying. With my sister marrying an American and this merger with an American company. San Francisco is our U.S. headquarters. Of course I will return to my home country to visit, but I feel as if this is my adopted home now. Come on,'' he said as if she was the one who was dawdling. ''Let's get this reception settled.''

As much as Tarik used his charm and persuasive powers and money, the second hotel was also unavailable for months. When Carolyn suggested making some calls instead of driving all over town, he insisted once again that his way was best. Face-to-face contact was how he preferred to operate. She pictured the search going on and on into the night until she dropped from hunger and exhaustion.

''You have no faith in me,'' he said as they drove down the steep hill toward downtown.

''I didn't say that,'' she protested.

''But you're thinking it. Your face gives you away.'' He reached over to gently touch her cheek.

Tarik knew he should keep his hands off the wedding consultant. But she was irresistible. Was it because she'd told him she was a virgin that made her so desirable? Every man wants to be the first in a woman's life. To be responsible for awakening her sensuality and teaching her the pleasures of physical love. Or was it just the charming way she blushed? Was it her soft skin and masses of curly hair?

No, it was more likely because they were on a mission together. He needed her and perhaps in some way she needed him. Only until the wedding was planned, then he could go back to business. In the meantime he felt as if he'd been let out of school early, been given a reprieve from business matters, and regained part of his lost youth. Was that all due to this woman? If so, he'd better get a grip on his emotions—the ones he didn't have. And keep his hands to himself.

"Here we are," he said, stopping in front of the hotel to allow the valet to park his car. "The St. Francis Hotel. I stayed here when I first came to the city. Before I bought the house. I ate at the restaurant on the top floor every night. Maybe they'll remember me." He could tell Carolyn was still skeptical by the way she looked at him. It wasn't her way of doing business, but it was his. He wanted to show her that it worked.

The manager did indeed remember Tarik. It could have been because of the generous tips he left. It could have been because they didn't get that many sheiks staying for three months. Whatever it was, he wasn't shocked when he heard the date of the wedding was only one month away. He merely nodded and looked at his appointment book. Then he escorted both of them to a private banquet room on the top floor with spectacular views of the city and the bay. "It's our newest facility," he explained. "I haven't scheduled anything here until July, but for you..."

"Thank you," Tarik said, nudging Carolyn gently. Hoping that she'd finally admit he'd been right.

"I know your family comes from a different part of the world," the man said. "And you say the groom and his family are American. So I would like to suggest a compromise for the reception. Something a little different. Neither American nor Middle-Eastern. I propose a Balinese theme with Gamelon musicians in the background. You'll need a different band for dancing of course, that's up to you."

"Of course," Carolyn murmured.

"The floor panels can slide back," the manager continued, waving his hand at the inlaid wood, "to reveal an oval lotus pool with a bamboo bridge. I suggest orchid and fruit displays by our resident decorator. Then the caterer could provide a sumptuous buffet and a gold-dusted tiered cake in the same motif.''

''What do you think?'' Tarik asked Carolyn.

''It's an interesting idea,'' she said, glancing around the room at the teakwood panels and the small tables decorated with flowers. ''Completely original. But will your sister...''

''Irrelevant. She's not here. We are. You and I are making the decisions.'' Tarik realized that only twenty-four hours ago he'd said ''I'' and now he was saying ''you and I.'' It gave him a strange feeling.

''Then I say yes,'' Carolyn said. ''Considering how little time we have. It sounds original and it could be very beautiful.''

The manager smiled. He asked how many guests and gave them an estimate of the cost. Tarik thought he heard Carolyn gasp at the figure, but to him it was a bargain.

''Won't you stay for dinner in the sky room, as our guests of course,'' the manager said.

Tarik was about to say yes when he realized he should consult Carolyn first. Consulting a woman went against the grain in every way. He was accustomed to giving orders, both in his personal and business life. He assumed he'd be giving them to the wedding consultant but it wasn't working out that way. She was the kind of strong-willed woman who wanted a say about everything, it seemed.

''I really shouldn't,'' she said. ''I have things...''

''It will give you a chance to sample our food. Of course it won't be the same as at the reception, but we're very proud of the quality. I think you'll find it meets your expectations. Our chef is very good,'' the manager said.

''I'm sure he is, it's just...''

Perhaps she had a date. Or perhaps she simply didn't want to spend any more time with him, Tarik thought.

He, on the other hand, wanted to spend more time with her. He knew nothing about her, except that she was a virgin and a wedding consultant and she wasn't married. She was a mystery that he wanted to solve. He also did not want to eat alone. It would remind him of those early lonely days in the city when he knew no one except his office staff. He'd take a file folder of work projects to dinner with him and pore over it between courses in the hotel dining room. He was no longer homesick or lonely but he didn't want to eat alone tonight. He wanted to eat with this woman he'd hired. He wanted to watch her face by candlelight, hear her talk and maybe even coax a smile out of her.

She didn't say anything for a long moment, and he had to stifle the urge to insist. To order her to eat with him. Though he knew it would be counterproductive. If she walked out, if she insisted on leaving, he'd have to go back to the office or back to the huge house where Meera would be cooking some of her native curry for herself. Neither appealed to him. She had to say yes. He wouldn't admit it, but for some reason he needed, wanted to have dinner with her.

"Well..." she said.

"Think of it as work. I know I do," Tarik said. "It's research. Nothing more, nothing less." He deliberately kept his voice businesslike. But he didn't feel businesslike. He felt young again, the way he did before he'd inherited the business, and looking forward to dining with her more than he should.

When she nodded, albeit reluctantly, he felt a rush of excitement as if he'd just hit the bull's-eye with his bow and arrow on his private archery range. It was the same jolt of adrenaline he got when he scored. He told her it was only research, he told her he thought of it as work, but he didn't. He loved his work. He found it satisfying to be a part of an effort to extract oil from the ground, to bring money to his homeland, to carry on a tradition of service begun by his grandfather. But having dinner with an attractive woman, a woman who intrigued him was not the same thing, not at all. It was something else. Something he didn't want to name. "You won't regret it," Tarik said with a smile. He just hoped he wouldn't either.

Chapter Four

The dinner was superb. The cuisine was better than he remembered. The company was better than he'd imagined. The soft candlelight made Carolyn's skin glow and her eyes shine, and he couldn't tear his eyes from her. Carolyn—that was her name, but she hadn't given him permission to call her that, so he hadn't. It probably wasn't a good idea to get on a first-name basis with her. Then she'd have to call him by his first name and where would that lead to? Before he knew it, he'd be asking questions. There were so many things he wanted to know about her. Did she have a boyfriend? Who did she live with? Why was she still a virgin when other American women were not? But if he asked, he would then have to answer her questions. She'd ask if he'd ever thought of marriage, what he was looking for in a wife—things like that—personal questions he didn't want to answer.

As it was, propriety dictated that he keep the conversation on a more impersonal level, so he asked instead about the weddings she'd planned, including the underwater ceremony with the professional divers where she had to outfit the guests with fins and snorkels. Not only did she smile, she laughed along with him when she described another bride and groom who got lost on the way to the reception because the groom, according to the bride, "refused to stop and ask for directions." Then there was the wedding of the bungee jumpers.

"At least my sister's wedding will not be as much of a challenge as theirs was, I hope," he said. "Though I imagine jumping off the bridge at the end of a bungee cord is no more risky than getting married, no matter how it is done. Taking a leap of faith, jumping off into the air, not sure if you're going to ever bounce back. I don't see myself doing it."

"Bungee jumping or getting married?" she asked.

"Either. They both require an enormous amount of courage," he said lightly.

"You don't strike me as being fainthearted," she said.

"Thank you," he said, though he wasn't sure she'd meant it as a compliment. "What I am trying to say is that I don't picture myself standing up in front of the whole world promising to love, honor and obey."

"Obey really isn't used much anymore," Carolyn said, looking at him over her coffee cup, her eyes slightly narrowed. "Not for many years. When my parents married, my mother promised to obey. He never let her forget it. Cherish is a word I prefer."

"So obey is out of style. Like Niagara Falls. Cherish is fine, but it's entirely different," he said. "Tell me what's wrong with obey." He set his cup down and leaned forward.

"Everything," she said firmly. "Obedience shouldn't be

a part of marriage. That implies that one person is the boss.''

''Of course. The man,'' he said.

She frowned. ''I prefer to think of marriage as a partnership.''

''Do you? Perhaps that is why you aren't married.'' He almost said *Perhaps that's why you are still a virgin.* But he stopped just in time. He hoped to make this a pleasant, impersonal dinner with no arguments, no hard feelings. It had been a long time since he'd sat across a white linen tablecloth having dinner with an attractive woman by candlelight. It might be even longer before it happened again. He would try not to spoil the occasion.

''I'm not married because I don't want to be married,'' she said. ''Not to a bully, that's for sure. Maybe your view of marriage as a union in which the wife obeys her husband is the reason *you're* not married.''

''I would never marry a woman who refused to obey me,'' he said. ''Call me a traditionalist, but that's how I am.''

''I would call you a chauvinist.'' Her eyes shot angry sparks at him.

''A chauvinist?'' He almost laughed. Was that the best she could do? It didn't bother him. He'd been called worse. ''You sound like a feminist,'' he said.

''I'll take that as a compliment,'' she said. ''I'm proud of being a feminist.''

''As I am of being a chauvinist,'' he countered.

''Now that we understand each other, I'll be leaving. I'm glad we've had this talk,'' she said, reaching for her jacket on the back of her chair. ''It was an excellent dinner. Thank you.''

"Don't thank me," he said standing to help her with her jacket. "Thank the manager."

He too was glad they'd had that talk. As lovely as she was to look at, as soft and sweet on the outside, he'd found out how headstrong and stubborn she was on the inside. Not the type he intended to marry if he ever did marry. She was about as far from his ideal as possible. She was the kind his father warned him about. And with good reason. As they waited for the valet to bring his car to the front of the hotel, he could still hear his father's words in his ear.

"Marrying a woman from a different background is a sure way to disaster and a lifetime of misery. Choose a modest woman who puts duty and family first. A woman who understands her place in the world. Duty is a concept foreign to American women. They are too independent. They're unpredictable and emotional also, undesirable traits in a wife. Find someone who has as much to gain from the union as you do. Whose family is compatible with ours. Who shares common interests and who will benefit from the marriage as much as you will."

He hadn't listened to his father the first time his father gave him that advice. And he lived to regret it. For the past ten years he had buried his emotions and devoted himself to the family business. He learned once and for all not to allow his heart to become involved. The next time he chose a woman for his wife, he would not stray from traditional virtues. Modesty, humility, deference and yes—obedience, too. Nothing wrong with that.

Straying was what got him in trouble the last time. So far this woman, this Carolyn, had not shown her emotional side, but it was no doubt lurking just below the surface and she was certainly too independent. Perhaps even too independent for an ordinary American man, which was why she wasn't married. It didn't matter. It didn't matter to him if she never married. If she remained a virgin forever. What mattered was that she was planning his sister's wedding, but so far it looked like he was doing as much planning as she was.

Of course she'd ordered the invitations and she was planning the honeymoon, but he'd have to supply the guest list at least. And he'd found the church and the reception site. Maybe he didn't need her after all. On the other hand there were still the flowers, the photographer and oh, yes, the dress. He definitely couldn't choose a dress without her. He'd just have to put up with her for one month.

When he dropped her off at her shop it was dark, and he insisted on walking her to her car. She looked annoyed.

"Most women would be grateful to have protection on a dark city street," he remarked acerbically when they reached her car.

"I'm not most women," she said, shoving the key in the lock of her car.

"How true," he muttered to himself. "Wait," he said as she got into the car and closed the door. He rapped on the side window. She lowered it a crack. He braced his hands on the frame. "I have some other issues to discuss with you."

"Not tonight. I…I'm tired. I've had a full day."

"Tomorrow morning at my house then?"

"I'm busy tomorrow," she said.

"Busy? Doing what?"

"Working on another wedding," she said. "I'll get back to you next Monday. I should have some information for you then."

"What about the weekend? Don't you work on weekends?" he asked.

"Not this weekend. I'm taking my mother to the cat show at the Cow Palace."

He frowned. "A palace...a palace for cows?"

She almost smiled. But she caught herself just in time and pressed her lips together. Just as she tried to catch herself from relaxing and having a good time at dinner. She was trying too hard to be a businesswoman, and he could tell it was a struggle. She had all the right feminine, womanly instincts, but she wouldn't give in to them. It was a shame. But none of his business. In fact, the more businesslike she was, the more likely it was he would pull off this wedding.

"The Cow Palace is not really a palace, not the kind you're used to," she said. "And there are no cows there, at least not at the moment"

"Then why..."

"It's a long story concerning cows and cowboys and rodeos. All I can say for now is that this Saturday there will be a cat show at the Cow Palace, which is really a very large arena where they have events like rodeos and such and I promised my mother I'd take her."

"She likes cats?"

"She's always wanted a cat but my father never allowed us to have a pet. Now that she's divorced..."

"Ah, the joys of being divorced," he said not even trying to hide his sarcasm.

"I never said divorce was an occasion for joy. Relief is probably more accurate, at least in her case. It was something I urged her to do and if you knew her you'd see how happy she is. Happier than she's ever been. She's out from under the thumb of a tyrant." She took a deep breath. "And now if you'll excuse me..."

Before he could react she was gone. Before he could tell

her he was perfectly willing to agree that divorce was a reasonable solution for certain situations. Yet another evening he was left standing in the street behind her shop watching her drive away without having completed the conversation. He had more to say to her. Much more.

He was not used to being dismissed this way. He had many things to talk to her about besides divorce American-style. There were the ongoing wedding preparations. He hadn't brought up the wedding at dinner because he almost forgot it was a business dinner, and he got distracted. He thought they'd have time later. Now it turned out there was to be no later. Not until next week.

Back home in the huge house above the sea, it was quiet. Too quiet. Even the ocean was quiet tonight. Even with the windows open he could scarcely hear the waves crashing on the rocks below. He wandered from room to room. Meera was either out or she had gone to bed. He went to his office and studied the papers his lawyers had prepared for the merger. But his mind wandered. He kept thinking of Carolyn.

He said her name out loud in the silence of the empty house. Rolled the syllables around his tongue. The next time he saw her he would ask if he could call her by her first name. After all, they would be working together for the next month. How long could they keep up this formality? They were in America, weren't they? The land of nicknames and first names and strangers telling each other to have a nice day. He wondered if she'd enjoyed the dinner as much as he had. He remembered how the candlelight was reflected in her eyes and had softened her features. The curve of her cheek, the tilt of her chin. Perhaps she, too, had forgotten it was an all-business dinner until they got to the coffee. It was all downhill after that.

Not that it mattered. The only thing that mattered was that she plan this wedding for him. But if she insisted on going to a cow palace to see cats when she should be working for him, how in the name of Allah could she make the necessary arrangements in time? Speaking of the wedding, it was time to check up on his little sister. He checked to see what time it was in Switzerland, then picked up the telephone and put in a call to the boarding school in Lausanne.

"Tarik," his sister said. "I'm glad you called. I'm out of spending money. I'm going to Paris this weekend with a friend and I want to do some shopping. Can you wire me a bank transfer?"

Tarik frowned. "Paris? I thought you were studying for finals." Carolyn's words came back to him. *Perhaps she could buy a dress in Switzerland* and his reply that she was too busy studying for finals.

"I am studying, but I've been studying so hard I need a break."

"Who's the friend?" he asked.

"No one you know."

Her evasive answer bothered him. It was his duty as her legal guardian and her brother to know who she was friends with, who she was traveling with. But this was not the time to argue over that when he had more important matters on his mind. "I've sent your plane ticket," he said. "The wedding is in less than a month, you know."

"Look, Tarik," she said. "I've told you before I can't marry a man I don't love. I don't even know him."

Tarik picked up a pencil and tapped it forcefully against the edge of his desk. What was it with these women and their romantic ideas? "Of course you know him. You met him and his family during your winter holiday. I explained it to you then and you agreed.''

''You explained it to me, yes. And I agreed that it was important for the companies to merge. I never agreed to marry a stranger. If you want the families to merge, then you get married.''

''If the Bransons had a daughter I would be more than happy to marry her.''

''Even if you didn't love her?'' Yasmine asked incredulously.

''There's no such thing as love,'' he said.

''I knew you were going to say that,'' she said.

He exhaled loudly. ''You know of course why Father married Mother?''

''Don't change the subject,'' she said. ''Theirs was an arranged marriage in another country and at another time. It has no relevance to me and my life. Or to yours. I advise you to stop meddling in my life and worry about your own.''

Tarik shook his head in exasperation. ''It is my job to take care of you.'' He carefully ignored the word meddle. ''Since our parents are both dead, I'm your legal guardian, and I will be until you are twenty-one. I've explained to you over and over the reason for this marriage, how important it is to our family and to the family business. It is what our parents would have wanted. You are young, Yasmine, and you don't know what you're saying. When I was your age I felt as you do. But now that I'm older...''

''Older? You're not that old. You're not old enough to give up on love. Just because one woman...''

''Just what do you think you know about love?'' he demanded, unwilling to discuss his own past. There was a long ominous silence. ''Who do you think you are in love with?'' he asked, suddenly more worried than he'd been since the merger was proposed.

''No one,'' she said lightly. ''I'm speaking hypothetically only.''

''Good,'' he said, only slightly relieved. She didn't yet understand how important duty and loyalty really were. But she would. And she would thank him in time for what he was doing. He didn't know she knew anything about his previous involvement with the American woman. It was the last thing he wanted to discuss with his little sister.

He let the pencil slide through his fingers and leaned back in his desk chair. ''I called to tell you that the wedding plans are going very well. I have the cathedral reserved as you know, and now I've hired a wedding consultant to take care of the other arrangements such as flowers and the dress and the photographer and...''

''Yes, yes, that's fine, Tarik. I have to go to class now. Goodbye.''

After she hung up so abruptly, Tarik looked at the clock. It was possible she had a class at seven in the morning in Lausanne, but it wasn't very likely. He retrieved the pencil and snapped it in half, venting his frustration only a little. What happened to the little girl who'd followed him everywhere around the compound, while he taught her to shoot with a bow and arrow and to swim in their pool.

Somewhere in the years between then and now he'd lost her respect. At least she hadn't out-and-out refused to marry Jeffrey. When she returned to San Francisco, she wouldn't have time to think. She'd simply get married and live happily ever after in a house he'd buy for them. Some day she'd thank him for what he'd done. Not that he wanted or needed her thanks. The merger and her happiness were all he wanted.

His satisfaction would come when the two families and the two companies merged and became as one to their mutual benefit. His sister would come to understand how lucky she was that he'd found her a suitable husband. Then and only then would he feel he had done the job he'd inherited from his father. He would make his father proud of him by completing the job he'd started years ago. The family and his country would benefit, just as his father had intended.

The noise in the Cow Palace was deafening. Nervous cats were meowing, and nervous owners were trying to calm them. "Mother, are you sure you really want to get a cat?" Carolyn asked.

"Why not?" Mavis Evans answered, peering into a cage that contained a small Angora. "I always wanted one. Your father didn't. So we never had one."

"I know, but is this the right time of your life to take on the responsibility of a cat? They need a lot of care. Feeding, brushing, cleaning up after..."

"Hmmm..." her mother said. "Sounds a lot like your father, except for one important point—cats are glad to see you when you come home."

"Do you mean that men aren't?" Carolyn said, absently petting a small friendly Manx.

"Some men, but don't marry a man to tame him, Carolyn," her mother said. "That's all I have to say."

"Don't worry, I'm not getting married any time soon."

"You're not meeting anyone, are you? You're in the wrong business. Have you thought of moving to getting into a different line of work or moving to Alaska? They say the odds are good there," Mavis said.

"The odds may be good but they also say the goods are odd. I meet enough odd men in my profession. Oh, no."

Across the vast arena of the Cow Palace, past acres of Siamese and Abyssinians and Persians, a tall man with a regal air was standing and scanning the crowd. Sheik Tarik Oman. Though he was wearing a casual sweater and slacks, he still stood out in the crowd, looking around imperiously as if all these cats were his subjects. She'd like to see him try to control them the way he tried to control everyone else in his life. What on earth was he doing there?

"What is it?" her mother asked.

"Speaking of odd men..." she murmured.

"Who? Where?" her mother asked, turning her head in his direction.

"Don't look now, but across the room is one of my clients. The tall one next to the podium."

"How nice. Shall we walk over and say hello?"

"No, definitely not. Come over here. Pretend we're interested in these Calicos." Carolyn crouched down to peek into their cage, but her mother continued to stand and stare across the room.

"What a handsome man," her mother said. "He doesn't look odd to me at all. Too bad he's getting married."

"He's not getting married, his sister is. Trust me, Mother, the whole situation is very odd and so is he. He doesn't see me, does he? He doesn't know I'm here, I hope."

"I don't think so. It wouldn't hurt to be polite, would it? I mean, how odd can a man who loves cats be?"

"But he doesn't. He's only here because..." Why was he here? Had he come looking for her because of some emergency regarding the wedding? Whatever it was it could wait until Monday. She refused to let business interfere with her days off. She needed a break from the intensity of his royal highness. "Or if he loves cats, they're only second to himself. He's a sheik."

"A sheik, a real sheik? That explains the air of confidence then," her mother said. "And the dark eyes and hair. He looks like he just got off the royal steed."

"Mother, your imagination is running away with you," Carolyn said "Tell me when he leaves." She shifted awkwardly on the hardwood floor. "My knees hurt and I'm seeing spots in front of my eyes."

"That could have something to do with the Calicos," her mother suggested.

"I feel like I'm getting a tension headache," she muttered. "Damn the man."

A few minutes later when she thought she couldn't possibly stay there on the floor, face-to-face with a bunch of Calico cats, for another second, she heard his voice.

"You must be Mrs. Evans, Carolyn's mother. Though you look young enough to be her sister, I see the family resemblance. How do you do, I am Sheik Tarik Oman."

Carolyn moaned softly. *Young enough to be her sister.* Where did he learn these things? Or did they come naturally to all sheiks? How did he even know she was there and how had he sneaked up on them? Why hadn't her mother warned her? And more importantly how was she going to rise gracefully when she had a cramp in her leg?

"How nice to meet you. My daughter has told me very little about you," Mavis said pointedly, nudging Carolyn with her toe. "Do you like cats?"

"Very much," he said. "But I didn't come to see the cats today. I came to see your daughter." He reached down and gallantly extended his hand. So he knew she was there all along. What could she do but take his hand and allow him to pull her to her feet.

Flushed and irritated that she couldn't take a day off without the sheik tracking her down and annoyed with herself for telling him where she'd be today, she crossed her arms over her waist and glared at him. If only she could forget how warm and strong his hand felt against hers.

"Yes?" she said.

"Forgive me for intruding on your day off," he said smoothly, his dark gaze including her mother, too, in his apology. "But I received a call from the cathedral this morning saying they had an opening this morning between weddings when the organist is available along with the deacon who will be performing the ceremony. It seemed a good opportunity to do a brief run-through of the ceremony with the music. Since they are usually booked solid on Saturdays, I agreed. It would be most helpful if you could come, too. If, that is, you could spare an hour or so of your time. After you've finished looking at cats of course."

"Go ahead, Carolyn," her mother said. "I can tell you've seen enough felines for one day. And I'm looking forward to the judging at three o'clock. You see," she said to Tarik, "I'm trying to decide what kind of cat to buy."

"Are you looking for a purebred or simply an ordinary tabby?" he asked. "A small cat or a large one, long or short-haired?"

"Well..."

"Mother hasn't decided, have you?" Carolyn asked.

"I have some suggestions," Tarik continued as if Carolyn hadn't spoken.

I'll just bet you do, she thought. She wouldn't be surprised to find he had suggestions and opinions on every imaginable subject. He proceeded to give her mother a rundown on the virtues and drawbacks of several breeds. While Carolyn watched and listened in amazement, her mother appeared to hang on his every word as if he were the world's expert. Did he really know what he was talking about, or was he trying to impress her and her mother? And if so, why?

"That's fascinating," her mother said, clearly in awe of both his looks and his encyclopedic knowledge of the subject. "How do you know so much about cats?"

"My father was fond of cats," he said. "Some lived outdoors, some in the house. I'm afraid he spoiled them all quite abominably."

"What happened to the cats when your father died?" Carolyn asked in spite of herself. In spite of the fact that she didn't want to engage in this conversation at all.

"The cats are well cared for," Tarik answered with a smile. "You can be sure of that. Father made the necessary arrangements before he died as he did with everything else."

"He must have been quite a thoughtful man," her mother said.

"It is my goal to live up to his legacy," Tarik said simply.

Her mother nodded and Carolyn could tell by the look in her eye that he'd won over yet another female. If only her mother could hear him giving orders, insisting on having his own way, making decisions for everyone including her who he'd hired to make decisions for him. But that didn't happen, at least not today.

"All right," Carolyn said impatiently. "But just an hour."

"Will you follow me in your car?" Tarik asked.

"My mother drove, so I'll have to ride with you." Now she'd be stuck with him and he with her, though the prospect didn't seem to bother him as much as it did her, if his benign expression was any indication. And he'd have to take her home afterward. She didn't like the idea of his knowing where she lived. If today was an indication, he'd think nothing of dropping in whenever he needed her.

They drove up Taylor Street to the top of Nob Hill, which in the last half of the nineteenth century was home to the men who had made their fortunes in gold mining and railroading. Now Nob Hill was covered with elegant apartment houses and hotels, like the ones they'd visited the other evening in their search for a reception site, as well as the impressive huge Gothic church where the wedding would take place.

Tarik parked in the church lot and they walked to the front of the church to admire the beautifully carved bronze doors of Paradise. Carolyn ran her hand over the smooth surface, admiring the quality of the work. Of course she'd been to the church before, but hadn't taken time to fully admire the many details of this San Francisco landmark and one of the nation's oldest cathedrals.

"Excellent reproduction," Tarik said. "Have you seen the original doors of Paradise on the Baptistery in Florence?"

"No, I've never been to Europe," she said.

"Never been to Europe?" he repeated. "But you must go. If only to acquire ideas for weddings. The lace in Belgium, the glass in Venice, the pastry in Vienna..."

"I suppose you've been there many times," Carolyn said.

"I go often enough on business to warrant keeping an apartment in Paris. It makes more sense than staying in a hotel each time."

"How nice," she said. "I understand how valuable such a trip would be for me, it's just..." How to explain to a man with limitless funds that she couldn't possibly find the time or the money to travel to Europe, no matter how beneficial to her career. No need to wonder how well he knew Europe, probably like the back of his hand.

"It's just that you are too busy at present," he finished for her. "Perhaps on your honeymoon. Oh, no, I remember, you are going to a deserted island where you can throw caution and your clothing to the winds and cavort in limpid blue water."

The way he looked at her, as if he could see her without her clothes, as if he knew how she'd look floating naked in aquamarine water made her feel breathless, as if she'd run up the steps to the cathedral. Carolyn bit her lip and turned away. She studied the doors once again, concentrating as hard as if she was planning to duplicate them in clay when she got home, but it was only to escape that all-knowing look in Tarik's dark eyes.

"I'm sorry," he said. "I've embarrassed you, Carolyn. I may call you Carolyn, I hope. Since we'll be working together. And you must call me Tarik."

She wanted to protest. It was so much safer being Ms. Evans. She'd never known what to call him. Tarik was easier than calling him Sheik or Your Royal Highness, so perhaps he had solved that problem for her anyway. Besides she felt foolish insisting on being called by her last name. So she didn't say yes and she didn't say no. But she knew he interpreted her silence as a yes.

They walked inside the cathedral and stood in silence, in awe of the classic architecture, the arched ceiling, the vast nave and the chapel. Strains of organ music floated through the air. Rehearsal for tomorrow's service, or perhaps for the next wedding.

"Do you have an appointment with someone?" Carolyn whispered, not wanting to interrupt anyone's private worship.

"With Reverend McClane," he whispered back. "Ah, there he is now."

A tall, portly man in a white robe approached them, introduced himself and instructed them in the details of the ceremony. He asked about music and Carolyn suggested several pieces for the organist to play while the guests assembled. Tarik had no objections to her choices, as well as the traditional wedding march and the recessional, and that much was quickly settled. Then the cleric suggested they do a run-through right there and then, taking advantage of the brief time between weddings.

"But we're not..." Carolyn began, afraid the good man thought they were the couple who were getting married.

But the man brushed off her protest and told Tarik to go to the altar and wait for her to come down the aisle. He told them the deacon was there and would run through the ceremony. Then he waved to the organist at the rear of the church to prepare to play the wedding march.

"Timing is very important," the minister said. "Of course we must take into account the wedding dress and the long train. That will add a few minutes."

Carolyn wanted to say that the dress hadn't been chosen so no one knew if it had a long train or not. "I really don't think..." she said, feeling distinctly uneasy at the idea of walking down the aisle of a church like the bride she wasn't with the sheik waiting at the altar. But before she could verbalize this thought, Tarik strode forward, and she was left behind. She gave a rueful glance at her khaki slacks and white sweater. She was dressed for a cat show not a wedding rehearsal.

When Tarik reached the altar, he turned and looked at her. If he ever did get married she knew he'd have that same solemn expression on his face. And how would his wife-to-be look? Pale, beautiful, wide-eyed? How would she feel? Nervous, jittery, with a fluttery feeling in her chest, just like Carolyn felt right now? The aisle looked as long as an endless highway. She'd never make it to the altar if her legs didn't stop trembling.

She told herself it was just a run-through. Not even a rehearsal. Not even *her* rehearsal. If it was her wedding, who would walk her down the aisle? Who would steady her nerves and tell her everything would be all right? She might have stood there forever woolgathering, if the organist hadn't started the music and the kindly minister hadn't come up behind her to nudge her gently and tell her it was time. Like a robot, she put one foot ahead of the other, her eyes riveted on Tarik's face.

So this is what it felt like to be a bride. All she needed now was the father, the flowers, the dress and the groom. The flowers and the dress were no problem. She knew where to get them. She'd supplied them for many brides, but the groom, that was another matter. She reminded herself that she was not a bride and wouldn't be any time soon and Tarik was not a groom and was not exactly on his way to the altar either. But she kept walking and approaching the altar and Tarik.

The way Tarik was looking at her made her heart pound. This was not real, she told herself. This was make-believe. This was a job. Then why did she feel as if time stood still and the whole world had stopped turning on its axis? That this is what it would be like if…if…

But it wasn't. This was make-believe. Instead of a wedding gown she was wearing khakis. Instead of a groom, it was Tarik at the altar, staring at her, his face a study in concentration.

"Four minutes," he said, looking down at his watch as she approached. "Can't you walk any faster?"

The mood was shattered just as surely as if he'd thrown a glass at a brick wall. But he didn't notice.

Carolyn clenched her jaw and joined him at the altar. "I'm sorry," she said under her breath so no one could hear but him, "but this is a once-in-a-lifetime walk down the aisle. It should not be rushed."

A man who was most certainly the deacon from the way he was dressed in a black robe and red mantle came down from the pulpit and joined them. He smiled benevolently at them as if they were the most wonderfully, ideally suited couple he'd ever married. Then he went through the traditional ceremony briefly, skipping the vows and the exchange of rings, but ending with "I now pronounce you man and wife."

For a long moment she and Tarik stood facing each other at the altar. The look in his eyes was unfathomable. She tried to drag her gaze away, but there was nowhere else to look.

Finally the deacon broke the spell. "You may kiss the bride," he said. Carolyn thought she'd collapse on the spot. This was going too far. Way too far. Though she thought he was informed as to the situation, the man must be under the wrong impression. They were not going to be married. They were stand-ins. She opened her mouth to explain this to him, but no words came out. All she had to say was let's go. All she had to do was grab Tarik's arm, turn and march back down the aisle. But she didn't. She couldn't move.

Why didn't Tarik say something? Why didn't he take her hand, tuck it under his arm and start walking? Surely he had no more desire to kiss her than she did to kiss him. Instead he leaned forward and angled his head so his lips were only a breath away from hers. He hesitated for a long moment. And she knew. She knew then he was going to kiss her. She knew she wanted him to kiss her. She also knew it was wrong. That if she had any sense she'd turn her head away and then his lips would land on her cheek. That wouldn't be so bad. That would be nothing to fear.

If he was going to kiss her, why didn't he just get it over with? The longer he stood there, the more intensely she felt the heat from his body in the cool air of the church. The chords from the organ still vibrated in the hushed silence. The sun shone through the stained-glass windows. The tension built until Carolyn couldn't stand it another minute. Just as she was about to bolt back down the aisle with or without him, Tarik finally closed the distance between them and kissed her. At first a brush of his lips across hers, clinging for a long, long moment, cutting off the light from those magnificent windows. Cutting off all rational thought also. Then a long deep kiss, but not long enough. Only long enough to tease, to tantalize her. To make her want more. So much more.

She took a deep breath and willed her voice to be steady. "Four minutes," she said lightly. "Can't you kiss any faster?"

"This is a once-in-a-lifetime kiss," he breathed without missing a beat. "It should not be rushed."

Touché, she thought.

Her knees trembled. If he hadn't taken her hand and tucked it under his elbow for the recessional at that moment, she might have.

"Go ahead," the deacon advised. "Now the pace can be quite brisk."

Tarik nodded and they marched back down the aisle toward the rear of the church.

She glanced at him, wondering if the kiss had really meant anything to him at all. *Once-in-a-lifetime kiss* was just a joke. She wondered if he'd felt anything at all. Probably not, if that grim expression on his face was any indication. Even if he did feel anything, he'd never admit it. After all, if he admitted to an increased heart rate or any other symptom, he'd have to head for the emergency room.

"I believe a smile is required," she said mildly with a glance at him. "The bride and groom are supposed to be deliriously happy. Is there any reason..."

"Why I can't smile? Of course not." He forced his mouth to turn up at the corners and gave what, on any ordinary man, would have been called a smirk. On him it looked ridiculous. So ridiculous, Carolyn's lips curled upward in spite of herself.

"Was that funny? Did I amuse you?" he asked, tightening his grip on her hand.

She nodded. "I hope your sister and her husband will be smiling more naturally."

"So you object that my smile is not natural. I'll try again. How's this?"

This time a beguiling slow smile creased his face. Natural or forced, the smile transformed his face. His jet-black eyes gleamed, his lips curved and he looked years younger and incredibly sexy. She reminded herself sternly this was playacting. On both their parts. But if the butterflies in the pit of her stomach were acting, they were doing a very good job of it.

They suddenly found themselves out on the front steps of the cathedral in the fresh air. Tarik turned to Carolyn, his smile suddenly gone.

"About the kiss," he said, his eyes narrowed. "I know

you thought it went on too long, but other than that, how was it?''

''It was fine, but...I don't really think it was necessary,'' she said, feeling the color rush to her face.

''Not necessary,'' he said. ''But enjoyable nonetheless.''

Enjoyable? she thought. That was not the word she would have chosen. Thrilling, exciting, dazzling, earth-shaking. That was more like it. Too long? Hardly. But she had to cover her feelings somehow. Being flippant was one way. She just didn't know if it had worked.

At that moment, the minister came through the bronze doors. He told them the rehearsal had gone very well. He said the deacon was pleased and would see them the day of the wedding. He made some suggestions and asked a few questions, all of which were answered by Tarik. Which was a good thing, because for some reason, Carolyn had nothing sensible to say. She simply couldn't concentrate on what the man was saying. The touch of Tarik's lips on hers lingered. She was still in a daze, but evidently the kiss hadn't made a lasting impression on him.

''What next?'' he asked.

''I have to go home,'' she said. The sooner the better. She needed a break from this man, as much time as possible away from him. ''You must have work to do, or don't you work on the weekends?''

''Yes, of course, but...'' Tarik glanced out toward the bay from the top of Nob Hill, taking in the sailboats bobbing in the water, the dark green islands of Alcatraz and Angel Island. Of course he had work to do. He always had work to do. And normally on the weekends that was exactly what he'd be doing. But with the wedding coming up he was distracted. Or was it the wedding consultant who had him even more distracted?

"Of course I have work to do and so do you. I've taken up too much of your weekend already," he said. "I apologize."

She looked startled. "I didn't think sheiks had to apologize for anything."

"How many sheiks have you known?" he asked.

She smiled. She had a lovely smile. He'd seen it twice today and he wished he could capture it on film or canvas. It was like watching the sunset over the Golden Gate. He had the feeling that no matter how many times he saw her smile, it would always have that effect on him.

"Just one," she said.

"So it is my fault that you have some kind of wrong impression of us," he said. "Perhaps I've been a bit overbearing at times. But it is only that I have many things on my mind." Those many things included her, unfortunately. It was her fault he was losing his focus. While he should be at his office, studying the terms of the merger, he was lingering at the entrance to the church, trying to think of ways he could prolong the encounter. Thinking of what excuse he could give for not taking her home yet. She appeared anxious to go home, but he didn't. He didn't want to go to his house, nor to his office. Neither seemed as appealing as spending time with Carolyn Evans. He wished she felt the same.

Kissing her had been a mistake. Perhaps he'd offended her. Kissed her too long? She could have pulled away, couldn't she? He hadn't forced her. For him the kiss wasn't half long enough. In all fairness, he'd given her time to turn away. She hadn't. Her lips were soft and warm and had only made him want to kiss her again. Longer and slower and deeper this time. To give her time to respond.

But would she? He could think of no more excuses to keep her with him. So he drove her home.

She lived in the part of the city called Cow Hollow. She explained that at one time in the eighteen-hundreds, there were dairy farms where charming Victorian houses like the one she lived in, stood today.

"So in America, cows not only have palaces, they have hollows also," he said as he drove down Greenwich Street toward her house.

"What about in your country?"

"No cows. Cows require grass and hay, which are in short supply in the desert. We do have camels though, but they are not allowed inside the palace. They are remarkable beasts of burden, able to withstand heat and sand and go for long stretches without water, and best of all, we can ride them across the sands where no other animal or vehicle can go. Your cows give milk, but I dare say they cannot be saddled."

"That's true, but cows are gentle and I understand camels are ill-tempered."

"They've been known to display some bad behavior, yes. But after a hard day, trekking across the Sahara under a blazing sun with a heavy pack on their back, perhaps they can be forgiven an occasional show of temper."

Before she could respond, he pulled up in front of her house and they both noticed her mother standing in front of her house with a cat in her arms.

"What on earth?" Carolyn said as she got out of the car. "What is she doing here?"

He, too, got out of the car to pay his respects, but before he could, Carolyn's mother rushed up to her daughter.

"Carolyn, I'm so glad you're home," her mother said, her voice tremulous, her forehead creased in a frown. "I got the cat, but the worst thing has happened. They won't let me keep him at my place."

"But why didn't you ask before..." Carolyn said.

"I never thought.... Other people in the building have pets," her mother said. Mavis Evans's lower lip trembled and the cat shivered pitifully as if he understood he might be homeless. "But as soon as the landlady saw me with Max she came running out and said they weren't allowed. Only those who had their pets when they moved in, and when those pets die, they aren't allowed to replace them. I thought maybe you..."

"No, Mother, no pets allowed here. I'm sorry. He looks like a nice cat." She reached out to pet the striped tabby with the grey body and black stripes. "And you've already named him."

"Yes, I looked and looked and asked a lot of questions just as you said, Mr...."

"Tarik. Please call me Tarik, Mrs. Evans."

"Tarik," she repeated with a wan smile. He could tell she was worried. Who wouldn't be with a brand-new cat and no place to leave him? He looked like a nice cat, too. Tarik felt all eyes were on him. Not just mother and daughter, but the cat too. They all seemed to be saying, what are we going to do now?

Chapter Five

"I'll move, that's what I'll do," her mother said.

"You can't move today, Mother."

"Well, I know, but..."

"In the meantime, I'll take him," Tarik heard himself say. He was almost as surprised as the other two by his offer. He certainly hadn't planned on offering to take the cat. The words came out of their own accord. Of course he was accustomed to living with cats in his father's house, but keeping a cat in the city would require some effort. But he said he'd do it, and once he'd given his word, he couldn't back down. He was rewarded for his spontaneous offer by the grateful look on Mavis Evans's face. Then Carolyn spoke up.

"You can't do that. You live in a mansion. He might soil your carpets and scratch your furniture. Where would you put him? Who would take care of him?"

"I'll take care of him. Let me worry about the details," he said. The woman just wouldn't leave well enough alone.

Here she was peppering him with questions he had no answers for. The truth was he had no idea where he'd put the cat. He could just imagine the reaction from Meera who already thought she was overworked. Nonetheless he was accustomed to succeeding in whatever project he undertook. There was no reason he couldn't care for a cat for a few days. Compared to a dog, they were self sufficient.

"I'll get a little cat house for him so he'll never have to come into your mansion," her mother said to him. "It would only be for a few days. I'll look for a new place to live tomorrow. Are you sure you don't mind?"

"Of course he minds, Mother. He's too polite to say so."

"Polite? That sounds like a compliment. Do you know that's the nicest thing your daughter has said to me," Tarik said.

Mavis looked from Tarik to Carolyn with a puzzled expression on her face. "I don't understand. That's not the way I brought her up."

"I'm sure it isn't," Tarik said. "You mustn't blame yourself. She must have gone astray after she left home."

"I'm standing right here," Carolyn said, glaring at Tarik. "There's no need to talk about me as if I wasn't here. I would prefer that you wouldn't talk about me at all, or at least until I've left. Which I intend to do as soon as possible. Mother, could I speak to you for a moment?"

"Of course."

"I mean alone."

Tarik noted that Carolyn's cheeks were pink and her voice had risen. He didn't know her very well, but he knew that she was upset with him. Because he'd offered to take her mother's cat? He thought she'd be grateful. He would never understand women. He watched them walk a few paces away from him and spoke in hushed tones while the cat snuggled into her mother's arms.

"You can't leave the cat with the sheik, Mother, he's my client," Carolyn said. "It puts me in a very awkward position."

"I'm sorry," her mother said. "It wasn't my idea. I'm just as surprised as you are. I mean I don't even know him. He must be trying to impress you."

"Don't you see?" Carolyn said softly with a glance over her shoulder at the sheik. "He's not trying to impress me, he's a control freak, just like Father."

"I don't see that at all," her mother said. "He seems like a kind, thoughtful person. Not at all like your father."

"That's because you don't know him," Carolyn muttered.

"Do you?" her mother asked.

"Well yes, I think I do. I know his type, anyway."

"How could you? You've never met a sheik before, have you?" Mavis asked.

"His being a sheik is beside the point. He has to have his own way. He has to be in control," Carolyn insisted.

"I need a place for my cat," her mother said. "I don't see that his offering to take the cat has anything to do with his being in control. What do you suggest I do?"

Carolyn shook her head, her arguments deflated. "I don't know. You have a problem, and I agree, you can't turn down an offer like that. I'm warning you though that with this man, one thing leads to another. I told him I was busy this weekend and here he is. He never gives up."

"That can be a virtue, in some cases," her mother said mildly.

"In this case it isn't, believe me." Carolyn looked from the cat to her mother to Tarik who was still standing on the pavement, looking remarkably patient. Finally she gave in. What choice did she have? She really didn't understand why he'd offered, and she really didn't want to know. Her desire to escape into her house, to be alone for the rest of the day, was stronger than ever, but impossible. She couldn't just leave her mother, the cat, and the sheik together to sort this out.

So after a brief discussion, it seemed logical that Tarik was to go home to prepare his housekeeper. Carolyn and her mother went to buy a cat house if there was such a thing, cat food and a litter box. The plan was for them to take the cat and his equipment to Tarik's house as soon as they had purchased the equipment.

Her mother strolled down the block carrying her cat and Carolyn leaned down to speak to Tarik through the side window of his luxury car. She braced her hands against the window frame, wishing he weren't so close. Wishing she weren't so aware of the fathomless depths of his dark eyes, so deep she could drown in them. Aware, too, of the small scar at the edge of his eyebrow. Wishing he wouldn't look at her the way he did, as if he knew something she didn't.

"Are you sure you want to go through with this?" she asked.

"Of course," he said. "The cat will be in the yard. Your mother can come by and see it and feed it, but otherwise he can take care of himself. It isn't going to be forever, after all," Tarik said.

"No, but I don't know how long it will be. Finding an apartment that will take a pet isn't going to be easy. Mother is a bit naive, I'm afraid. You see for years my father did everything. Made all the decisions, handled the money, took care of everything."

"As a husband should," he said.

"You see? You don't understand. Marriage should be a partnership. If it had been she would have had her cat years ago. But it wasn't. He wasn't just the boss in our house. He was king. The rest of us were just his servants."

"No, I don't understand," Tarik said with a frown. "But the past is the past. We must deal with the situation as it is in the present. We will find a way because we must. She wants to keep the cat and she shall."

We? Did he say *we* must deal with the situation? *We* will find a way? How did he get involved with them anyway? She blamed herself. Knowing that if only she hadn't told him she was going to the cat show none of this would have happened.

"Oh, she certainly does want to keep it," Carolyn said. "But that doesn't mean you have to take it in."

He shrugged. "Then who will?"

He had her there. Who indeed?

"It's settled," he said. "I have the space, and I'm taking the cat."

Yes, she thought. He had the space, he had the money, he had the servant, he had the power to do whatever he wanted. It was impressive, it was also a little overwhelming. Carolyn did not want to be overwhelmed. Why couldn't her mother see the resemblance between him and her father? Truthfully she was having a problem seeing it herself at that moment. All she could see was the look on his face. Not proud, not arrogant, he looked like an ordinary man for once. An ordinary man with more money than he knew what to do with, an ordinary man who was movie-star handsome and was going out of his way to be kind to her mother. Why?

"It pleases me to be of service," he said as if he'd heard her question. "I was brought up that way."

"Noblesse oblige," she murmured.

"Exactly," he said. He covered her hands with his. The warmth from his broad fingers spread and went straight to her heart. She tried to pull away but he held her hands where they were. But more than his hands, it was his gaze that held her. The silence stretched between them. She tried to think of something to say. If she pulled hard enough he'd have to let her go, but she couldn't. She couldn't tear her eyes away either. She wanted to stay that way forever. The memory of his kiss in the church came back to haunt her. Did he remember it, too? Did it haunt him, too? She'd never know.

Finally he took his hands away, broke eye contact and started the engine. "I'll be waiting for you," he said.

She stood on the curb with her arms wrapped around her, hugging herself to keep warm in the fading daylight as his car disappeared down the street.

"Fancy car," her mother said as she came up behind Carolyn. "How much money *does* he have?"

Carolyn shrugged. "I don't know and I don't care as long as he pays his bills. He's just a..."

"I know," Mavis said. "He's just a client."

Carolyn knew her mother would be impressed with the mansion. She was even more impressed when the huge iron gate at the entrance swung open as if on command, upon their approach in her mother's car. Carolyn remembered that she'd driven through the gate and parked in the driveway. Was that only two days ago?

"This is his house?" her mother asked in hushed tones.

"One of them," Carolyn answered.

Tarik was waiting for them. Instead of calling a servant, which Carolyn imagined a sheik would do, he untied the so-called cat house himself from the top of the car, lifted it off and carried it to the corner of the yard where it seemed most naturally to fit.

"But Tarik," her mother said, after he'd instructed her to call him that and not *sheik* or *Mr. Oman,* "this is a garden. What if the cat eats your flowers and chases birds?"

"What can you expect?" he asked. "Cats will be cats."

Carolyn had to admit the cat seemed deliriously happy in the sheik's garden. And who wouldn't be? It was full of blooming rhododendron plants with dense oleander bushes around the periphery. There was a small pond with lily pads and a brick patio. The air was fragrant with the scent of flowers mingled with the salt spray from the ocean far below. Carolyn couldn't help but think what a lovely spot it would be for a wedding. It was nothing personal—it was just how she viewed the world—from the eyes of a wedding consultant. She wondered if it had occurred to Tarik to have his sister's reception at home.

"This is far too good for a cat," Carolyn said to Tarik as her mother filled the cat's dish with the high-performance cat food she'd purchased.

"I'll be the judge of that," Tarik said. "It's time the yard got used. I never come out here. Now I'll have an excuse."

"Won't it take you away from your work?" Carolyn asked.

"Sometimes I need a break," he said. "Sometimes I get too immersed in things like the wedding and the merger. There are so many details."

"I thought that was why you hired me, to take care of the details, at least those of the wedding."

"I thought so, too, but the closer it gets, the more I get

involved. I must confess I'm enjoying participating in certain details more than I thought.'' The look in his eyes told her just what details he was referring to. She bit her lower lip thinking of the kiss. The endless kiss that was over too soon. In spite of the cool ocean air sweeping up from the sea below, Carolyn felt the heat from his gaze, the heat from his body. And yet she shivered.

''You're cold.'' He took his hand-knit sweater off and wrapped it around her shoulders. He tied it loosely over her chest, his hands brushing lightly across her breasts. She took a deep breath to steady her nerves and wiped her damp palms against her khaki pants. How many times had he touched her today? How close had she come to making a fool of herself by blushing and falling apart at the seams? The wool sweater was warm and soft and smelled of leather and fresh sea-washed air and something that was uniquely Tarik. She wanted to bury her face in it and close her eyes. ''Come in for a drink of something warm, won't you?'' he asked.

''Oh, no. I must get home,'' she said taking a deep breath of cool air. She told herself not to weaken. Not to go back into that beautiful house. Not to let her mother even see it. She knew just what she'd think and what she'd say. Something in the order of *it's just as easy to fall in love with a rich man as a poor man.*

''We've taken up entirely too much of your weekend as it is,'' Carolyn added. And he'd taken up too much of hers, she thought. Pretty soon she'd have no life left except for the sheik's wedding and when it was over—all the hoopla and the excitement of hotel dinners and run-through rehearsals at Grace Cathedral—she'd be back to her old life. Which wasn't that bad, she told herself. Making people happy. Making their dreams come true. She squashed that little voice inside her that asked what about her, what about her dreams. Those dreams were not relevant. Those dreams didn't pay the bills.

She hustled her reluctant mother away from her new cat while her mother was promising to find a new apartment as soon as possible, in between telling Tarik how grateful she was, how much in his debt she was...until Carolyn thought they'd never get through the huge iron gate and back onto the road.

"Did we really have to leave so soon?" her mother asked plaintively as she drove away from the house on the seacliff.

"We really did," Carolyn said. "I know you'd like to spend more time with your cat, but you can come back tomorrow. Tarik gave you the combination to the gate, didn't he?"

"Yes, he did." Her mother gave her a long look then turned her gaze back to the road. "He's quite something, your sheik."

"Mother, he's not my sheik. He's not anybody's sheik. He's his own man. I told you..."

"I know what you told me, but I know what I saw. I saw the way he looked at you. He's interested in you. I don't know why you're not more interested in him. He's handsome, he's rich and he's unbelievably kind. I can't believe you were hiding from him at the cat show. Unless you're afraid of your own feelings. There comes a time in life when you have to let go of your fears, take a leap into the unknown and take a chance."

"Is that what you did when you married Dad?" Carolyn asked.

Her mother's face fell.

"I'm sorry. I didn't mean that."

Her mother took one hand off the wheel and patted her daughter's knee. "Never mind. I asked for that. Yes, I took a chance and let go, and I'm the first to admit I made a terrible mistake. But do you know what? I learned a lot from being married to your father. I learned what to look for in a man. And what not to look for. Call me a hopeless romantic, but if the right man came along today I'd get married again. But, back to you and your sheik, Carolyn, you have to admit you've never met anyone quite like him."

Carolyn shook her head. What good did it do to remind her mother again that he wasn't her sheik. Her mother said it all—she was a hopeless romantic when it came to men. Never met anyone like him? Oh, yes, she had. But this was not the time to remind her mother of the similarity between her father and the sheik. Her mother just couldn't or wouldn't see it. It was clear to Carolyn the sheik was a dictator. A benevolent dictator, but a dictator nonetheless. "You're right about that, Mother. I've never met anyone like him."

Her mother smiled and pulled up in front of the Victorian house where Carolyn rented the top floor. She kissed her mother on the cheek and congratulated her on getting a cat and got out of the car.

"Remember what I said," her mother called before she pulled away. Carolyn nodded, but she didn't know what she was referring to. There had been so much advice. All of it in regard to you-know-who.

She'd been in her apartment for at least five minutes before Carolyn realized she still had the sheik's sweater tied around her shoulders. And her mother never said a thing. Neither did the sheik. They both let her walk out with it. She untied it and flopped down on her soft, nubby oatmeal-colored couch and gave in to fatigue and pent-up frustration. She covered her face with the soft wool and let herself be immersed in the scent of the man. A warm rush of desire flooded her body, leaving her trembling. Good thing she was lying down or she would have fallen.

She groaned. What did the sheik want from her? What did she want from him? The answer to the first question was simple. He wanted her to plan his sister's wedding. The answer to the second question? She wanted to plan his sister's wedding. Period. If she wanted anything else, anything more, she was an idiot and a fool. The man didn't believe in love, for heaven's sake. She'd forgotten to tell her mother about that. That would have stopped her suggestions cold.

Don't marry a man to tame him. Her mother had said that.

Carolyn tossed the sheik's sweater across the room and headed for the bathroom where she ran a bath in the old-fashioned, claw-footed porcelain tub. Immersed in the hot water, she felt the tension slowly leave her body. She was finally able to relax. Until her cell phone rang.

She shouldn't answer it. It was bound to be something that would spoil her mood. That would jolt her out of her repose. But she did. She reached across to the vanity and picked up the phone. It was Tarik.

"I forgot to tell you something in the excitement of the cat's arrival," he said.

What was it about the sound of the man's voice that had made her heart pound like a jackhammer? She rested her head against the end of the tub, slid deeper into the water and told herself to calm down. "How is he?" she asked.

"Fine, just fine. He's sitting at my feet right now, looking extremely content."

"At your feet? Are you outside in the yard?"

He chuckled. She'd never heard him chuckle before. Didn't know he could laugh. The sound sent waves of heat through her body that had nothing to do with the temperature of the water.

"I'm in the library," he said. "The fog came in and I couldn't leave the cat outside."

"But he's a cat. He has a fur coat. He has a house..." She stopped. The little house couldn't really compare to Tarik's mansion. Even the cat knew that.

"He's very well-behaved," Tarik said. "He hasn't laid a claw on the furniture or peed on the carpet."

"I'm glad to hear it, but..."

"I thought I shouldn't have a cat in the city, but I see it's no trouble at all."

"Is my mother in danger of losing her pet?" she asked.

Again that deep-throated, husky chuckle. "Not at all. One of these days I'll get one of my own. What I'm calling about... Am I interrupting something?" he asked.

She sat up straight in the tub. Maybe she hadn't given him enough credit. He had manners, she'd have to admit that. It was just that he only used them when he wanted to. "No, not at all."

"I thought I heard a splash."

"Yes, I'm... I'm...in the bathtub." As soon as she said the words, she knew she shouldn't have. Why hadn't she said she was washing the dishes? Or her car? There was a long silence. Her whole body turned pink. Of course it could have been the hot water. But it wasn't. It was his voice. It was the picture she had of him sitting in his library, his legs stretched out, a fire in the fireplace, a cat at his feet. So normal, so virile, so masculine, so...so...endearing. She didn't want to be endeared. She wanted to keep her original impression of him fresh in her mind.

"I see," he said, his voice turning rough around the edges. She had the feeling that he *could* see, all the way across town, all the way into her bathtub. But that was impossible.

"The reason I'm calling," he said slowly and deliberately, "is that I have the guest list for you. I'll drop it by tomorrow morning."

"But tomorrow's Sunday. I'm not working tomorrow," she protested. "The invitations haven't been delivered yet. So I wouldn't be able to address them anyway." Even as she said the words she felt guilty. If she didn't address invitations, there were other things to do. With the wedding only a month away, she should be working on it every single day. While she hesitated, she knew he'd be within his rights if he reminded her that she owed him big-time for keeping her mother's cat. Maybe he was too polite to do that, but he really didn't have to say a word. She knew she was in his debt. The debt weighed heavily on her shoulders.

"All right," she said. "I'll meet you at my office tomorrow."

"Why don't I come to your house?" he asked. "If you're not going in, it would save you a trip."

Her house. He would come to her house. Was there no place to hide from the sheik? No day to rest up from his presence, to shore up her resistance, to get a break from his relentless dark gaze, his mesmerizing voice and his imperial manner?

She sighed. It meant cleaning the house from top to bottom. And what else? How else to return the hospitality of a sheik? Would she have to prepare tea and cakes? No.

This was America. She would make coffee. Period. Hopefully he'd have something else to do afterward. He'd hand over the list and leave. But meetings with the sheik seldom turned out the way they were planned. They seemed to go on and on. The best way to prevent that was to plan something of her own. But what?

They agreed he'd come by at eleven o'clock the next morning and she hung up. By morning she had it all planned. She'd meet him at the door dressed in spandex shorts and a T-shirt for a run on the Marina Green. Sheiks might ride camels across the desert, they might swim in their own pool every morning, but she felt fairly certain they didn't run for pleasure. She didn't either. Still, she knew it was good for her so she'd bought the right clothes and had all the right intentions, but had never actually gone running on the green. She knew she should go. Not only was it good exercise, it was a great stress reliever. So they said.

The minute he arrived at the door, she knew she'd made a mistake. His gaze raked her up and down, lingering on the tight shorts and the snug T-shirt. But what choice did she have? Appear in a full-length Hawaiian muumuu?

"I...I'm going running," she stammered, unnerved by the look in his eyes.

"You run?" he asked, rocking back on his heels.

"Yes, oh yes. That is, whenever I get a chance." It wasn't an out-and-out lie, it was just that she hadn't ever got a chance. That was the reason she hadn't been running. "I mean it's such a beautiful day so I thought..."

"Then I'll join you," he said.

"You run?" she said, so surprised she almost fell over.

"I ran cross-country in college at Berkeley. I had always been somewhat fleet-footed, but I didn't know it was an organized sport over here. As a foreign student, joining the team was a good way to make friends. It was either that or soccer.''

''Of course.'' She should have known. There was no escaping him. The only thing that could save her was that he wasn't dressed to run. She didn't say anything, but she glanced pointedly at his tailored slacks and polo shirt with some sort of emblem on the pocket. The royal crest, no doubt.

''I always keep my duffel bag in the car with my Nike running sneakers and shorts,'' he said. ''I never know where and when I'll need them. This is most fortunate. We can talk as we run.''

Talk as they ran? Carolyn would barely have enough strength to run, let alone enough breath to run and talk at the same time. Besides, what exactly would they talk about? She shouldn't worry. The sheik always seemed to have something to say. What worried her was that he'd see how slowly she ran.

Reluctantly she invited him in. She might as well. He expected it and she'd spent the morning vacuuming and dusting. He gave her the guest list and accepted her offer of coffee, then proceeded to look around her living room.

''It must seem small to you,'' she said, setting his cup on the end table. It seemed smaller than ever to her with this broad-shouldered man taking up so much space.

''Small but charming,'' he said. ''Like its owner.''

Out of anyone else's mouth it would have sounded phony. But somehow the sheik could get away with it. It might have been the way he looked at her, his gaze so steady, so unwavering. It might have been the serious tone of his voice that said he meant every word. Or did she just want to believe him. In any case, the way he scrutinized her made her cheeks flame.

She looked away hoping he wouldn't notice the effect he had on her, but the sheik noticed everything. Her mind raced, thinking of a way to change the subject. There were so many problems yet to be solved regarding the wedding, but at the moment she couldn't think of a single one. Oh, yes, the gift registry. So she asked him if the couple was registered. He didn't understand the concept until she explained.

"A good idea," he said. "Friends have asked me what to get them for a wedding present. Tell me how to do it, and I'll register them."

"But do you know the couple's taste well enough to choose their china, their glassware and so forth?"

"With your help."

"But I don't know them at all. I've been hoping to meet Mr. Branson, your sister's fiancé. At least..."

"Yes, yes, in good time. For the moment he's out of town on business. In the meantime here's my sister's picture you asked me for. For the newspapers."

"Oh, my, she's beautiful," Carolyn said, looking at a heart-shaped face with huge dark eyes.

"Yes, I believe she is," he said seriously. "Especially her smile. You remind me of her sometimes, your smile and your joie de vivre. She, too, is a romantic, which is why I am so confident the wedding will go off without a hitch with you planning it. She'll be so happy with the arrangements. And the gift selections. Tomorrow would be convenient for me to visit the stores with you and establish these registries you mentioned."

"I thought you were busy working on the merger."

"There is nothing more important than the wedding. Without the wedding there is no merger."

"Doesn't that put a lot of pressure on your sister?" she asked.

"Why should it?" Tarik asked. But when he thought of his last conversation with his sister he had to admit he was concerned. He stood and paced the small room while he spoke. "Royal families are accustomed to pressure. Or they should be. Pressure to succeed. Pressure to do the right thing. We are brought up to accept responsibility and whatever comes with it. Yasmine knows what is expected of her."

But did she? She'd always been headstrong and willful. Now more than ever. Perhaps she did feel the pressure of the impending marriage, and she was reacting in her own way. But when the time came he was sure she would come through and do the right thing. She had to.

"Enough wedding talk," he said. "If I may intrude on your hospitality, I will change into my running clothes in your house."

She was gracious enough to let him use her white-and-black-tiled bathroom to change in. He glanced at the old-fashioned bathtub and imagined Carolyn in it as she was last night when he called. The image of her floating naked in hot water, her breasts breaking the surface caused a flood of red-hot desire to slam into him like a renegade oil derrick. He clenched his jaw in an effort to stop the overwhelming desire for a woman he shouldn't desire at all.

He looked into the mirror and gave himself a stern talking to. Not out loud or she'd hear him. He told himself it was all right to admire her looks. It was only normal. She was beautiful in a wholesome American way. But it was not all right to kiss her no matter how good it felt. The minute he saw her this morning he'd had an overwhelming desire to kiss her again. It was wrong because kissing Carolyn was addictive, and he couldn't afford an addiction of any sort. On the other hand it was all right to admire her talent for wedding planning. To be grateful to her for helping him get through this difficult period. It was all right to spend time with her if the activities were work-related. But where had the line between work and play become blurred?

It had been a long time since Tarik had played at all. That was the problem. Since the death of his father, he'd been immersed in the family business. There had been no time to enjoy life. Now suddenly he seemed to have taken leave of his senses. He'd taken in a cat, temporarily of course, but quite unnecessarily. He'd enjoyed a leisurely restaurant dinner with Carolyn, also unnecessary. Now he was going running on a Sunday when he should be at home working. What happened to his willpower, usually made of iron? How had it failed him?

They walked from her house to the Marina Green. Then after the obligatory stretching, they ran on the paved walkway, with acres of green grass on one side, the sea wall on the other. There was a cool breeze off the bay, and a spectacular view of the Golden Gate Bridge. But the view that captivated him the most was the view of Carolyn running next to him, her hair tossed by the wind, her cheeks pink from exertion and her trim, firm body. He forced himself to look at the Bay and the bridge, but his gaze kept returning to the woman running alongside of him. He slowed his pace so they were side by side.

"Do you come here often?" he asked.

"Yes, whenever I get a chance," Carolyn said, panting. She'd come to sit on the grass and watch the boats on the bay. But not to run. He must realize that by the way she was huffing and puffing. "But not often enough. As you can see, I'm having trouble keeping up with you," she said pressing her hand against her chest. "I should run more often, it's such good exercise, but I get busy at work and I let the job come between me and a fitness routine. Obviously I'm out of shape," she said breathlessly.

"Nonsense, you're in excellent shape," he said, keeping his tone neutral, his eyes straight ahead. Good shape was putting it mildly. Her shape was beyond compare. Just because she was a slow runner didn't mean she wasn't in good condition.

"You are, too," she said politely. He noticed she didn't look at him. She hadn't looked at him since he came out of the bathroom in his shorts and T-shirt when she'd blinked and looked away.

"We must do this more often." There he went again. Inventing more ways to see her. As if they didn't have enough to do. And even after the stern talking-to he'd given himself.

"After I recover. I don't usually run this fast. I had no idea you ran. I'm afraid I'm slowing you down. Of course after the wedding, you'll have time to run more often."

After the wedding. He would have no excuse to see her again. Ever. Which was just as well. She said *I'll* have more time for everything. Not *we.* She knew as well as he that they'd never see each other again. She must be relieved. But he wasn't. He was afraid he'd miss her. Miss sparring with her, miss watching her blush, miss her company.

Maybe he'd come running by himself after the wedding was over. Why not? It was exhilarating, refreshing and good for him. Maybe he'd run into her, quite by accident. But would she be glad to see him? He was afraid not. Afraid he'd demanded too much from her. Too much o her time and her energy. They slowed down, and after another stretch, they headed back to her apartment. One way to get there was to take Union Street where her shop was located. She didn't appear to be in a hurry and he'd quite conveniently forgotten anything he was supposed to be doing.

Union Street was filled with Yuppies shopping at expensive boutiques. When they passed her shop, they stopped to look in the window.

"I almost didn't come in that evening," Tarik said, remembering the sight of all the wedding finery, the acres of sample flower displays, model wedding cakes and honeymoon destination posters. But most of all remembering the sight of Carolyn seated behind her desk, speaking earnestly with her clients, her hair a vibrant copper under the ceiling lights. And then she'd looked up and smiled at him.

"Are you glad you did?" she asked casually, studying the display in the window of her shop as if she'd never seen it before.

"Of course. I could never have done this wedding by myself. I know that now."

"But the city is full of wedding consultants. Why me?"

"You came highly recommended," he said. But it was more than that. It was the moment she looked up from the clients that night and met his gaze. There was something about the way she looked at him that prevented him from following his first inclination, which was to turn and walk away. From going to find another wedding consultant, the kind he was looking for, the one with twenty years of experience and thick ankles.

Once he'd seen Carolyn and she'd smiled at him, he knew he had to have her. As a wedding planner, of course. Nothing more.

"I'm afraid I behaved rather impulsively that evening," he said.

"That's putting it mildly," she said. "I haven't seen those clients since."

"But that's terrible," he said. "I must do something about that. Shall I call them and apologize?"

"No, never mind," she said. "I have too much work to do as it is."

"Then you must allow me to compensate you for the money you lost."

"It's all right," she said.

"No, it isn't. I insist."

"We can discuss it later," she said.

"Over dinner," he suggested. He didn't want the day to end. Didn't want to go back to his huge, lonely house which had never seemed lonely or huge before he'd met her.

She looked startled at the suggestion of dinner. "I can't," she said.

"Why not?" he asked. "Do you have another date?"

"No, no dates," she said and he breathed a sigh of relief. Why? It was none of his business.

"No boyfriend?" he asked. "Or fiancé?" He had to know. If she was attached he wanted to know now.

She shook her head.

He stifled the urge to ask why not. It was none of his business and she might be offended.

"Well, if you won't let me buy you dinner, let's at least stop for a drink. If only to replace the fluids we lost while running."

Before she could say no, he steered her into the next sidewalk-front café. They sat opposite each other across a small wrought-iron table. He ordered an iced coffee, she ordered an Italian soda. The sun warmed his back and turned her hair to flame. He leaned back in his chair, as if afraid he'd be burned, and studied her face. The urge to ask was overwhelming.

"May I ask why not?" he asked. "Why doesn't a woman like you have a boyfriend or a fiancé?"

Again the color tinted her cheeks. She obviously didn't receive enough compliments to become accustomed to them.

"It's the nature of my job," she said. "The only men I meet are already taken. My mother thinks I should find a different job where I'd meet more men."

"What would that be?" he asked.

"I suppose I could join the army, or become a telephone line repairman."

He smiled at the image of Carolyn in camouflage or a hard hat at the top of a telephone pole. "That sounds rather drastic."

"Not as drastic as moving to Alaska. That was her other idea."

"I thought Alaska was full of polar bears and ice caps," he said.

"Polar bears and ice caps and bachelors. The odds of men to women are twenty-five to one, I understand," she said.

The idea of Carolyn besieged by twenty-five men was a disturbing one. He hoped she wasn't taking her mother's suggestions seriously. "But you'd have to leave your charming shop. You obviously like what you do and everyone says you're good at it."

"I've always loved it," she said a bit wistfully. "It's a rewarding job, making people's dreams come true."

He leaned back in his chair and observed her thoughtfully. "What about *your* dreams?" he asked. "How will you make them come true?"

Chapter Six

"Come now," he said after a long silence. "Don't tell me you have no dreams. Everyone wants something they don't have."

"Do you?"

"The merger and the wedding. The wedding and the merger," he said.

"In a few weeks you'll have those things."

"If all goes well," he murmured.

"Why wouldn't it?"

He shrugged. He couldn't tell Carolyn about his sister. About the worries that kept him awake at night that she would back out of the wedding. Talking about it with her would solve nothing. He must try to think positively. "There are loose ends," he admitted. Loose ends—to say the least. "You didn't answer my question. What do you want? What about marriage and a family? Wouldn't you like to be planning your own wedding instead of those of others?"

"Yes, of course, some day. But as I explained, it's rather hard to find Mr. Right in my line of work. And I'm not going to change jobs or move to the frozen North to find him."

"Perhaps he'll find you."

She nodded but she didn't look convinced. Instead she pulled a flyer from her back pocket. "Here's something for you," she said, handing it to him. On the glossy pages were photos of thatched-roof cottages on a blue-green lagoon. Smiling local women in native costume offered tropical drinks to tourists in hammocks.

"Ah," he said. "The honeymoon. Yes, I can picture you there." He could picture her only too well. Her shapely body clad in only a bolt of flowered material knotted at the waist. The image made his heart feel like someone had kick-started it.

"Not me," she said. "Your sister and her husband. Is it suitable for their honeymoon? Do you think they'd like it there?"

"Would you?" he asked.

"Yes."

"Then make the reservations."

"All right. Now I really must be getting back," she said. This time they walked briskly and said goodbye at the door.

From her third floor window, Carolyn watched Tarik pull away in his car. She was glad she was alone at last. Every muscle in her body ached, though she wouldn't have admitted it to him for the world. She would admit that running and talking at the same time with Tarik had been invigorating and not as hard as she'd imagined. She'd been keyed up, adrenaline flowing, enjoying the fresh air, the beautiful views across the bay and yes, watching Tarik run so smoothly, so effortlessly. But that was then, this was now. She glanced across the room and saw his forgotten sweater. She groaned. How could she have neglected to give it to him?

She could have avoided this whole encounter if only she hadn't made up the story about going out for a run. By doing so she'd found out more about Tarik—more than she'd wanted to know. She had to admit he was an amazing person. When she heard him say he'd run cross-country at college she couldn't believe it. It was too late to say she was off to play basketball instead. Knowing him, he'd probably played basketball in his former life as well. No wonder the man had such a well-developed body. He was an athlete. Along with being a businessman. It served her right for trying to put one over on him. It never worked.

Her stomach growled. Reminding her she could have been dining with Tarik instead of facing an empty stomach and an empty refrigerator. But having another dinner with Tarik was not a good idea. She had the distinct feeling he wanted more than just the planning of the wedding. The looks he gave her. The questions he asked her. The remarks he made. Or were they just part of the sheik's repertoire? Just something all sheiks learn at the mother's knee? How would she know? She'd never met another sheik, and she'd never meet another one, that was for sure.

So she'd dine on peanut butter on crackers and soak her tired and aching body in a hot tub. And this time she would not answer the phone. And she would not feel sorry for herself. It was her decision to eat crackers instead of rare rack of lamb at some wonderful restaurant where the waiter hovered over the sheik because that's just what people did around him. That's what made him so insufferable, he was used to servants fawning over him.

That wasn't fair. She knew it. He was not really insufferable as she'd first thought. She was just trying to talk herself out of this infatuation with the sheik. She was seeing too much of him. To be fair, she had to admit his housekeeper Meera didn't appear to fawn over him. Just the opposite. And though he was oozing with self-confidence, he wasn't above hauling equipment into his garden and allowing a stranger's pet into his home.

Why shouldn't he be self-confident? she asked herself as she dragged her body into the kitchen to rummage through the refrigerator for a can of diet cola. She munched on a stale cracker as she toted up his accomplishments. He ran, he swam, he ran a huge company and what else? She didn't want to know. She just didn't want to succumb to his charms.

At first she thought he had no charms. But that wasn't quite true. At least according to her partner Lily and her mother. But what did they know? They weren't spending the major portion of their days and evenings with the sheik as she was. She was glad to have the evening off. Glad to be alone in her apartment with nothing to eat. Of course she was. She'd see the sheik tomorrow when they went to sign up his sister at a gift registry. She knew she must have other things to do tomorrow for the other upcoming weddings on her schedule, but for the life of her all she could think of was Tarik and his sister's wedding. This was not good.

Before she stepped into the bathtub she carefully turned off all her phones. But as she lay soaking in the hot water, she wondered if he was trying to call her, and if not, why not? Uh-oh. She was losing it.

She went into the office early the next day to get organized and to try to pull herself together. She made calls, but no one was in. She made lists of things to do and realized she was dreadfully far behind on everything, including some major items on Tarik's sister's wedding. She thought of calling him to ask about the rehearsal dinner, the band, the dress and the bridesmaids, but she didn't. He'd probably be in his pool right now. She closed her eyes to try to forget how he looked in his swimsuit, but the image wouldn't go away.

Fortunately Lily came in. Carolyn was grateful for the distraction, but unfortunately Lily only wanted to talk about the sheik.

"What's new with the sheik's wedding?" she asked.

"The sheik's *sister's* wedding," Carolyn reminded her. "I'm worried. This is the strangest wedding I've ever planned."

"Stranger than the circus clowns who got married under the big top, stranger than the bride who carried her tiny Lhasa apso down the aisle instead of a bouquet?"

Carolyn sighed. "Those were pretty strange, but at least the bride was around. I feel like I'm operating in the dark here."

"What about the sheik?" Lily asked. "Isn't he being helpful?"

"If you call taking up my weekends being helpful, I guess so," she admitted. "If you call providing room and board for my mother's new cat, I guess so. But as for the wedding..."

"Wait a minute," Lily said. "Back up. I'm lost."

Carolyn had to recap the weekend for Lily. Lily's eyes widened and she shook her head in amazement. "The whole weekend," Lily said. "You spent the whole weekend with this man, and it doesn't sound like it was all business." She gave her partner a knowing look that Carolyn tried to ignore. "What's going on here with you two?" she asked.

"Nothing," Carolyn said. "So don't look at me that way. The only thing that's going on is I'm planning a wedding for a bride and groom I've never met. Which has created certain special problems," Carolyn said, standing and walking back and forth between the display of model wedding cakes and stacks of fashion books. "Instead of helping me out, the sheik is a distraction. I'm way behind on this wedding. What was I thinking?" She raked her hand through her curls. "I never should have agreed to do a wedding in a month. Do you know I don't even have the invitations out yet."

Before Lily could answer, the phone rang. Carolyn let Lily answer though she knew, somehow she just knew, who it would be. Lily held the phone out.

"It's for you," she said.

Carolyn's heart started beating way too fast because of a simple phone call. She took a deep breath and told herself to calm down.

"I thought we should get an early start," Tarik said after he wished her good morning.

"I have a list of things to do," she said, going back to her desk.

"So do I," he said, "have things for us to do. That will last all day. The first is breakfast."

"I've already eaten," she lied. There was no way she was going to start off the day, start off the week with breakfast with the sheik. Dinner had been bad enough. The way he'd looked at her across the table. Making her feel special, like she was his date. As if he'd be dating a bridal consultant. As if he'd be dating anyone at all. But breakfast would be worse. There was something more intimate about breakfast. Something you don't do with a business client. Breakfast should be shared with someone you cared about. Someone you had feelings for.

Maybe the sheik was lonely. Maybe that's why he'd offered to take the cat. That's why he was inventing reasons to see her. But she wasn't lonely. She had her mother. She had her friends. And she had her job. A job she loved, she reminded herself. A job that required her full attention. Now.

She had to avoid any more meals with the sheik, as well as unnecessary meetings. There were enough things they had to do together without adding more. She ended up agreeing he'd pick her up at ten, and they'd see how much of a dent they could put in their respective lists starting with the wedding invitations and moving on to the department stores.

When she hung up, Carolyn stared out the window, reminding herself this was a man who put business first, who didn't believe in love and if he ever did get married, he'd marry someone who had connections or would help him in his business or someone chosen by his family. Though, in his family, it seemed as if he was the one doing the choosing.

"Carolyn, Carolyn..." Lily said. "No need to ask who that was. I swear, the man has cast a spell over you. I can see why. He's gorgeous, rich and he's coming on to you like gangbusters."

Carolyn snapped out of her reverie. "No, he isn't. You've got it all wrong."

"Don't tell me it's all business. I don't believe you. I've seen you handle the most difficult weddings without losing your cool. This is something different."

"You think I've lost my cool?" Carolyn asked incredulously.

"Some of it. And I think you're in danger of losing it all. Completely."

Fortunately there was another call, this time for Lily, that cut off any further conversation. Because this was an argument Carolyn knew she couldn't win. What Lily didn't know was that just the sound of Tarik's voice had the power to make Carolyn lose her cool. Of course she always got it back. In time. At least so far.

The next call was from her mother asking if she'd come for dinner that night. She said yes immediately. She'd have the perfect excuse if Tarik suggested dinner. Not that it was likely. After a day of running errands with her, he'd most likely be tired of her by tonight. But would she be tired of him? That was the question.

Their first stop was to pick up the invitations, the second was to bring them to Tarik's office on the top floor of the Wells Building where his secretary would address them. Carolyn knew he was rich. She knew he was important, but she still wasn't prepared for Tarik's office with its spectacular wraparound views of the city. His desk was almost as large as her kitchen. His staff as large as a battle regiment. She imagined he probably treated his employees like soldiers, too, giving orders the way he had the first night she met him.

As soon as he appeared he was deluged with messages and besieged by people waiting to see him. He left Carolyn with his smartly dressed, fifty-something, gray-haired secretary while he went to see someone.

"I won't be long," he said with a backward glance over his shoulder.

"It must be a great job being a wedding consultant," the secretary said as she set the invitations and the guest list on her desk. "Tarik says you're the best."

"You call him Tarik?" Carolyn asked, surprised.

"Oh, yes. I've been with him for years. And it's very casual around here. Especially since his father died." She glanced up at a portrait of the old sheik in ceremonial dress. Carolyn decided this picture was even more impressive than the one in Tarik's library at his house.

"The atmosphere changed," his secretary continued, "and Tarik has put his own stamp on the company. Even though he's a sheik, you'd never know it. He's a great boss. Very thoughtful. He never asks you to stay longer than he does, or to do anything he wouldn't do himself. So I can't complain."

You'd better not complain, Carolyn thought. *Not if you want to keep your job.* Still the woman's praise seemed genuine.

"When he got us together we all hoped it was his engagement he was announcing."

Carolyn bit her tongue to keep from telling her that Tarik would never marry unless it was financially advantageous. Unless he found a wife he could dominate completely. Surely this secretary who knew him so well knew that. Or had he fooled her? No, he would only marry if it helped the company, his country or his family. He didn't believe in love, he believed marriage was a duty. If she'd been with Tarik for such a long time, she must know that. If she didn't, it wasn't up to Carolyn to tell her.

"It's time for him to settle down," the secretary said. "If his father was here..."

"I suppose his father would arrange something for him," Carolyn said.

"I think his father stopped arranging things for Tarik after he interfered the first time. But he'd certainly encourage him to find someone suitable. To look a little harder. But he's not the type to drop everything and pursue some woman, especially after what happened."

Carolyn waited, hoping she'd go on and say what had happened, but Tarik came back and they left. There were still messages piled on his desk, his voice mail was overflowing and a line of people were waiting to see him. But Tarik said the wedding came first. Carolyn couldn't argue with that.

An hour later, the two of them stood in the middle of the fine china and glassware department of Gumps, the elegant store just off Union Square with a helpful clerk, clipboard in hand, by their side. The shapes and patterns, the dazzling array of beautiful place settings on tables were just a blur to Tarik. Fortunately Carolyn seemed to know what questions to ask. Unfortunately he didn't know the answers.

What were his sister's favorite colors?

How many place settings did she want?

Everyday dishes?

What pattern of silver?

He preferred looking at Carolyn instead of silverware. He could tell she was concentrating on the many choices by the way she drew her eyebrows together and bit her lower lip.

"Which one?" she asked, holding up a tray of teaspoons.

He forced himself to look. "That one."

She nodded. "I like that one, too."

They proceeded on to candlesticks, goblets and juice glasses, then dinner plates and stainless steel flatware. Fortunately, they agreed on every one.

The clerk beamed at them. "I've never met a couple who had the exact same taste before," she said.

Carolyn opened her mouth to explain they weren't a couple, but the facts were so strange and unusual she decided not to.

"You have no idea," the clerk continued, "how many couples argue over every little thing. I sometimes wonder how they're ever going to make it through life. Now you two seem perfectly suited. I wish you every happiness."

"You've been very helpful," Carolyn said quickly. It was either that or tell her *they* weren't getting married, it wasn't *their* wedding and these weren't *their* gifts. As far as every happiness...that was another matter.

Out on the street, Tarik put his hand on her elbow protectively. Instead of protesting, she gave in and let him guide her across the street. He must know by now she was not a fragile flower who couldn't take care of herself. So why remind him? She decided to relax and let him play the gallant role he was so good at.

"It is remarkable," he said as they crossed the street to the parking garage, "how similar our tastes are."

"I guess it is," she said, "considering we're complete opposites. I just hope we've chosen the right things."

"Don't worry," he said. But she did. She worried about his sister's reaction to the reception, the honeymoon, the gifts and the dress—to the whole darn wedding that had been planned without her.

"Have you heard from your sister lately?" she asked.

He frowned. "No. It's hard to get in touch with her because of the time difference. Either she's asleep or in class or..." He didn't finish his sentence. Carolyn had the feeling he was holding back information about his sister. Something she might want to know. "She has her plane ticket.

She'll be here on time,'' he said. But there was a look in his eyes that belied his confident words. Carolyn stifled the urge to ask, *but what if she isn't?*

They got a lot done that day, but not enough. There was still so much more. It had been a good day. A busy day. They'd had lunch on the run, hot dogs from a stand on a street corner.

''These are delicious,'' Tarik pronounced with surprise.

''You've never had a hot dog?'' she asked. ''You went to college here, didn't you?''

''Yes, but I lived with friends from my country. We had a cook.''

''I should have known,'' she murmured. ''What about pizza, tacos, donuts?''

''Of course. I've tried them all. I haven't been living in a cave, you know.'' He cocked his head and studied her face. ''Hold still,'' he said and reached over to run his thumb over her lower lip.

She felt as though he'd touched a live wire somewhere inside her. Every nerve ending went on alert. It was just his thumb. It was just her lip. But her body told her it was more than that.

''Just a trace of mustard,'' he explained matter-of-factly. But there was nothing matter-of-fact about the look in his eyes. Lunchtime crowds swirled around them on the corner of Sutter and Stockton Streets. She didn't see or hear them. All she saw was Tarik. When he took his hand away she gave a soft sigh of regret.

But that was five hours ago. They'd been busy every minute since. She looked at her watch and told Tarik she had to go. He said he did, too. She was relieved he didn't ask her to dinner. Relieved, but also a little disappointed.

Had he given up on her? Did he have a date? He didn't say.

She changed into comfortable drawstring Capri pants and an oversized white cotton shirt and drove to her mother's. Before she left she put Tarik's sweater on the table next to the door. She'd forgotten to return it today. She resolved to give it back to him the next time she saw him, which would be the day after next when they went to the bridal salon to look for the dress. Until then it would stay there, reminding her of how he'd wrapped it around her shoulders to keep her warm. Reminding her to return it.

There were delicious odors coming from her mother's kitchen. Mavis was a great cook due to years in the kitchen experimenting with recipes that would please her demanding husband. It smelled like *boeuf bourguignon* tonight. Her mother's eyes were sparkling. Her face was flushed with the heat from the stove.

"Have a good day?" her mother asked.

"Fine. I spent the whole day on Tarik's sister's wedding. But we got a lot done. The china is chosen, the invitations..." Out of the corner of her eye, Carolyn saw the small dining table was decorated with candles and flowers and set for three. "Who's coming to dinner?" she asked, truly puzzled.

"Didn't he tell you?" Mavis asked.

Carolyn took a deep breath. "You don't mean..." Her mother wouldn't invite him, would she?

The doorbell rang. A minute later Tarik appeared in the doorway, wearing immaculately pressed slacks, a polo shirt with another hand-knit Irish wool sweater over his shoulders. He smiled and handed her mother a bouquet of flowers. Her heart banged against her ribs. If only someone had told her she could have prepared. Somehow.

"Mother," Carolyn said under her breath. "You didn't."

Chapter Seven

"Why didn't you tell me you were coming here to dinner?" Carolyn asked Tarik after her mother had poured two glasses of sparkling apple juice for them, then excused herself to return to the kitchen.

"I thought you knew," he said blandly.

"No, I didn't."

"This is a nice place," he said looking around at the homey furnishings accumulated over a lifetime. "Your mother has excellent taste. As do you."

"You say that because as the saleswoman said today, we have the same taste."

"There is that," he conceded with a wry smile.

"Why are you here?" Carolyn asked.

"Because your mother invited me," he said, sipping his juice slowly. "I'm grateful for the opportunity to have a home-cooked meal."

"What about Meera?"

"She doesn't like to cook so she calls herself a housekeeper."

"Oh," she said. Who would have imagined the sheik would want a home-cooked meal when he could afford to dine anywhere he wanted every night. It made her feel guilty for not inviting him herself. As well as turning his invitation down to dine with him last night.

"Well," she said, uneasy with the sight of the sheik so at home in her mother's armchair, "I'll just go see if my mother needs any help."

She closed the kitchen door behind her. "How could you?" she asked her mother.

"How could I not?" her mother asked, giving the French stew a stir with a ladle. "The man has taken in my cat. I've tried to pay him, but he won't hear of it. I mentioned dinner and Carolyn dear, he positively jumped at the chance. Of course that may have had nothing to do with my cooking and everything to do with your coming tonight."

"This is so embarrassing," Carolyn said, running her fingers through her hair. If she'd known, she would have dressed more carefully. Painted her nails... No. He'd seen her windblown and frazzled. There was no point trying to fool him. Or impress him. "What if he thinks I put you up to it? That I told you to invite both of us to dinner?"

"I'm sure he doesn't think anything of the sort." Her mother looked shocked at the very idea. "Especially after seeing the look on your face when he walked in the door. Now, could you take the rolls out of the oven while I toss the salad?"

The dinner went more smoothly than Carolyn could have imagined. They talked about everything from her mother's cat, who was doing fine, to customs and food in his country, which were fascinating, to his and her favorite vacations. One of hers was on the Russian River where as a child she'd paddled a canoe under low-hanging branches and swam in fresh, cold river water. Which prompted Mavis to clear the table and get her photo album from the bedroom.

"Mother, I'm sure Tarik doesn't want to see a lot of pictures of our family," Carolyn said, shooting her mother a desperate look. There was nothing more boring than being subjected to someone's family pictures.

"But I do," he said.

"They aren't that interesting," she said, fidgeting with her napkin in her lap. She'd gotten through the evening so far without embarrassment, but this was going too far. They sat in silence until her mother returned, put the album on the table and retreated to the kitchen to make coffee. Tarik moved his chair next to hers. His arm brushed against hers. She should have moved away, even an inch or two would have done the trick, but she didn't want to. The warmth of his body, the smell of the natural wool of his sweater and the soothing aftereffect of a delicious dinner made her feel warm and contented and on edge at the same time.

On edge because she didn't know what he was going to o next. Probably he'd just look at the pictures. He'd make olite comments because he had to and then he'd go home. But what if she leaned against him and put her head on his shoulder? The thought was tempting. His shoulder was so close, so big and so strong. If she did, would he put his arm around her and hold her tight? Would she bury her ace in his sweater? Would he even kiss her again? No, of course not. The first time was only because they were play-cting in the church. A kiss was required.

She flipped the pages of the album, but he forced her to low down, asking reams of questions about the house they ived in, the friends and relatives. He paused at a picture her in a formal dress taken at a dance.

"You look lovely," he said, staring transfixed at the picture.

She covered her embarrassment by getting up to refill his glass. When she returned he was staring at a picture of a young Carolyn wearing braces. She tried to turn the page, but he put his hand over hers and held it there. Then he turned to look at her straight teeth. Or was he looking at her mouth?

She wondered if he thought about kissing her again the way she thought about it every few minutes. But apparently he really was only interested in observing her teeth. "Those wires on your teeth worked," he said. "You have perfect teeth. And a beautiful smile."

She took her hand from his. "Thank you," she said.

On the next page there was a picture of her father.

"He doesn't look so bad," Tarik said.

"You don't know him," Carolyn said.

"Does your mother keep in touch with him?"

"Oh, yes. She says he's much better now. He appreciates all the things she did for him. Like giving up the best years of her life to wait on him hand and foot." She realized a bitter tone had crept into her voice. "They didn't get a divorce until I went to college. She should have done it years earlier."

"It sounds like she's forgiven him," Tarik remarked.

"She has, but I haven't," she said flatly.

She felt Tarik's eyes on her, his unspoken questions hanging in the air.

If your mother has, why can't you forgive and forget?

Why keep him out of your life?

What did he do that was so terrible?

She didn't want to talk about it, so she was glad he didn't ask the questions out loud. She closed the album. He nother came in with the coffee and an inquisitive look on ıer face. If she thought this was a good idea throwing her laughter at a wealthy sheik, she was mistaken. Carolyn had alf a mind to tell her Tarik's views on love and marriage s soon as he left. But she didn't get a chance. Her mother old Tarik she was on the trail of a new apartment and ıanked him again for keeping her cat. Then she brushed ff Carolyn's offer to help clean up and Carolyn left at the ame time Tarik did.

"Do you know how rare that was?" he asked as he valked her to her car. She'd given up protesting his over-rotectiveness. She decided against telling him it was a safe eighborhood and she was unlikely to be attacked in front f her mother's building. It wouldn't change his ways. And ıst possibly there was something about his attitude that ade her feel safe and secure. Maybe she was starting to ıjoy being looked after. Which was a scary idea. What ould happen when he wasn't around? Would she be ner-ous alone on the street at night? Heaven help her!

"What was rare?" she asked, realizing he was waiting r an answer to his question.

"Sharing dinner with a family. I've never been invited an American home before."

"Really? Maybe people think that you dine on pheasant ıder glass every night, and they don't dare invite you to eir humble abode to share an ordinary dinner."

"There was nothing humble about your mother's abode ordinary about that dinner. Did your mother teach you cook as well?"

She wondered if that was a hint. If he wanted to be vited to her place next. Better let him know that was not ely.

"Actually I don't really cook much. I get something to

eat on Union Street then I usually go back to work in the evening,'' she said. ''Why don't you hire a cook?''

He shrugged. ''It seems a waste to cook for one person.''

''Exactly,'' she said. ''Good night, Tarik.''

He put his hands on her shoulders and before she could duck or turn her head he kissed her, cutting off the light from the streetlight and cutting off all rational thought. She thought she'd be prepared for his next kiss, she thought she could handle it. But she couldn't. She felt her knees buckle. He caught her and held her tight against his body.

He slid his tongue between her lips, and she moaned in the back of her throat. She supposed the whole neighborhood could hear her but she didn't care. All she cared about was Tarik. All she wanted was for him to continue his barrage against her senses.

When he finally pulled away she was dazed and aching for more. She wrapped her arms around her waist.

''I've been wanting to do that all day,'' he said in a rough voice. ''I couldn't let you go until I had.'' He took the keys from her icy fingers and opened her car door. ''Drive safely,'' he said as she slid into the driver's seat.

She nodded, unable to speak. As she glanced up at her mother's window she thought she saw the curtain move. How was she going to explain this? How many people had seen her kiss a sheik on the sidewalk? Just one was enough. Especially if that one person was her mother.

When she got home she had a message from her mother waiting on her machine. She just knew what she was going to say. She could imagine her glee at having thrown her daughter to a bonafide sheik then watching while they kissed in front of her building. But her message had nothing to do with the kiss. It had to do with a missing photo from her album.

"It's the one of you at your first prom. Did you take it?" her mother asked.

"No, of course not. It probably fell out of the book, and it's on the floor somewhere," Carolyn said.

"Probably," her mother said.

But Carolyn knew what had happened and so did her mother. Why didn't he ask if he wanted the photo? "I don't know, maybe Tarik took it for some reason. I told you that was what he was like. He's used to getting what he wants. So it's just possible that he took it," she said.

She was annoyed. She was flattered. Why did he take the picture? It was old. She was young in it. She didn't really look like that anymore. And what was she going to say about it? Nothing. It was best to say nothing. Pretend it never happened. Maybe it hadn't. Maybe the photo really had fallen on the floor.

"Never mind," Carolyn said. "It doesn't matter."

The next day Tarik called to say there was an emergency at one of their oil fields. They'd had to shut down because of a breakdown of some equipment and he was flying back home. She gripped the phone so tightly her knuckles turned white. She didn't say anything, but the questions swirled around in her head.

How long will you be gone?

What about the wedding?

How will you fix the problem?

What if you don't come back?

"I don't know how long I'll be gone," he said, as if he'd read her thoughts. "But I know you'll carry on with the preparations without me."

"Of course. No problem," she said. A wedding consultant is always prepared for emergencies. A wedding consultant must remain calm while all around her are losing their heads. But there was a problem. There was more than one problem. There were dozens. Of course she could make the selection of a dress and a band and flowers and the rings by herself, but she didn't want that much responsibility. It was bad enough doing it without the bride and groom. But doing it without the brother of the bride was daunting. But what could she say? Don't go. Stay here. Let the oil wells take care of themselves? Obviously not.

He asked her to tell her mother that Meera would feed the cat, and then he said goodbye. Carolyn stared at the phone for a long moment before she called him back and offered to take him to the airport. Of course he'd probably say he'd call a taxi. But he didn't. He accepted immediately and seemed genuinely touched by her offer.

"That was very thoughtful of you," he said, when she pulled up in front of his house. He lifted his small valise into the trunk of her compact car. "I could have called a cab."

Thoughtful? If she'd been thinking she would have let him go in the taxi. She needed a break from him. The longer the better. Especially after that kiss last night. Now her heart was pounding and her hands were frigid. Nerves. He made her nervous. Besides, she had work to do.

"Sometimes the taxis aren't reliable," she explained. More to herself than to him.

"This is more efficient," he said. "And more pleasant. I never know what to say to taxi drivers. Whereas I always have something to say to you." He smiled, and she felt as if the sun had broken through a cloud.

She was going to miss him. Despite what she told her mother, despite the fact that this relationship was going nowhere, she felt the attraction and so did he. She told herself that opposites attract. But if they were opposites, what about their having the same taste? She told herself he was getting to be a habit. Because of the rush job they were doing, they'd been together almost constantly since he'd first walked into her shop.

"I must apologize for kissing you last night," he said.

She swerved to avoid a cyclist who came out of nowhere. She told herself to concentrate on the road and not on the passenger.

"The street is not the proper place to kiss," he added.

"I don't think anyone objected," she said.

"Not even you?" he asked.

"I found it enjoyable," she said primly, purposely repeating his comment after the kiss in the church.

"Is that all?" he asked.

She didn't know what to say to that. She could hardly tell him it was thrilling, exciting and memorable. Surely he knew that by the way she'd reacted. If she told him, it would go right to his head.

"I can't afford to get involved with a man like you," she said, fixing her eyes on the road ahead. "We come from two different worlds." She didn't say that his world seemed exotic and fascinating to her. That it made her world seem ordinary and humdrum.

"What kind of man are you looking for?" he asked.

"I'm looking for someone who respects me, who considers me his equal, who shares my values and my goals."

"Who will love, honor and obey you, I know," he said. "I'm sorry, I mean cherish."

"That's right."

"You don't have to tell me what you're looking for," she said. "Someone to obey you but not love you because you don't believe in love." She glanced at his profile, at his stubborn jaw, proud nose and high cheekbones. She wondered if he'd deny it. He didn't.

"I'm much too busy to look for a wife," he said. "Perhaps I should have allowed my father to find me one as he offered. One with a similar background and one who shares my values and goals. I didn't do a very good job of finding my own."

She remembered his secretary saying *after what happened...* She wondered if she'd ever find out what did happen.

"Did you try?" she asked.

A long silence. Finally he spoke. He spoke slowly, choosing his words carefully and deliberately. "There was a young woman at my university. Very beautiful, very intelligent, very American. I thought I was in love with her. Now I know it wasn't love at all. It was only infatuation. My father saw it. He knew it. He warned me that a marriage of the heart would never work for someone like me. A sheik must marry out of duty, not love. I didn't listen. I thought I knew everything. The arrogance of youth. It turns out my father was right. I gave up everything for her and then she turned around and broke off our engagement. I never spoke of it and my father never said a word, but he knew. Of course he knew." Tarik's voice dropped to where she could barely hear him.

"I'm sorry," she said. She had the feeling the girl broke off more than their engagement. She'd broken his heart too. Carolyn wanted to reach over to touch him, but she didn't dare.

At the airport she let him out at the curb. Before he got out he leaned over and kissed her. A brief brush of the lips. Nothing to get excited about. It meant nothing. Only goodbye. But all the way back to her office, she felt his lips on hers. All the way back she thought she could hear him say what he'd never admit, that his former fiancée had broken his heart. He never said that it still hurt. But she knew it did. It was there in his voice.

When she got back to the office, her mother called. She didn't tell her she'd taken Tarik to the airport. That would give her mother the wrong idea. As it was, her mother was far too excited about him. She called to say that Tarik had sent her a bouquet of flowers with a thank-you note for the dinner.

"What manners," her mother said. "He's too good to be true. He'd be quite a catch for some lucky girl. Aren't you glad you didn't go to Alaska to find a man? There probably aren't any sheiks up there."

Carolyn groaned. "Maybe I should have. I'm not looking for a sheik, you know. Just an average, all-American Joe. If and when I do get married, it will be to someone who's sweet and kind and who's looking for a partner instead of a servant."

"Maybe I'm wrong," her mother said, "but if a sheik is looking for a servant, I'm pretty sure he'd hire one. I don't know what your sheik is looking for, I only know what I saw."

Did that remark refer to the embrace on the street in front of her apartment? Carolyn didn't want to ask. Didn't want to hear the glee in her mother's voice. Didn't want to hear her say I told you so. She said goodbye and went back to work. Tried to go back to work. But she'd been working on Yasmine's wedding so intensively she forgot what else she had to do. She could continue to work on the wedding, but it wouldn't be easy and maybe Tarik would be back in a few days. She could only hope. For the sake of the wedding plans of course.

But after a week spent trying to focus on other jobs, she kept thinking about him. Remembering how his kiss had caused her to forget where she was, forget that he was the last man she wanted to get involved with, manners or no manners. Remembering the things he'd said, the picture of his house on the sea and the way he looked in his running shorts.

Even Lily noticed Carolyn was distracted.

"You've been staring at that picture of wedding dresses for a half-hour," Lily noted one morning.

"What? Yes, I know," Carolyn said, closing the most recent issue of *Bride Magazine*. "I don't know what to do. How would you like to pick out a dress for a bride you don't know, never even seen?"

Lily shook her head. "Impossible, I'd say."

"Impossible, but necessary. Tarik claims his sister has no time to choose her own dress. Does that sound right to you?"

"Never heard of a bride that busy. But there's a first for everything. First time you've ever met a sheik, right?"

"And the last I hope." One sheik was enough in anyone's life.

Lily nodded as if she agreed, but Carolyn was afraid she didn't realize the effect the sheik had had on her.

"Seems kind of quiet around here without him popping in or calling. Don't you miss him?" Lily asked.

Miss him? Carolyn didn't want to admit how long the days seemed, how boring life was without him and how often she thought about him. "A little," she said. "But that's normal considering how much time I was spending with him. Only because of the wedding, of course."

"Of course."

Carolyn got up from her desk and grabbed her jacket

"I'm going to the florist. At least I can pick out the flowers by myself. I don't think he'll mind. I just hope he likes hydrangeas, roses and amaryllis as much as I do. It's the strangest thing, the sheik and I have pretty much the same taste. So far anyway."

"Hmmm, that is strange considering how different you are. Although I think you exaggerated a wee bit," Lily said. "From your description I was expecting an ogre."

"Well? Didn't you see how he insisted he come along with me that day? He dragged me all over town on errands we could have done by phone. Then forced me to have dinner with him."

Lily bit back a smile. "Forced you to have dinner at the St. Francis Hotel? Oh, I feel for you. How mean can a sheik get?"

"That's not all," Carolyn said, ignoring her partner's remarks. "Then he insisted on taking in my mother's new cat."

"No wonder you're upset. No wonder you can't concentrate. No wonder he's driving you crazy."

Carolyn paused on her way out the door and surveyed her partner. "I'm no stranger to your sarcasm, Lily, and I know what you're trying to say. Okay, I admit I might be overreacting. But I'm telling you, I'm just glad it isn't the sheik who's getting married."

"Right," Lily said with a long look at Carolyn. "Not yet anyway. What if he meets someone while he's back in his country?"

Carolyn's heart lurched. What if he did? What if he met someone submissive and obedient, who wouldn't object to promising to obey him? Someone with similar values and goals. "Then I guess I'd be planning his wedding next," Carolyn said lightly. But she wouldn't. She couldn't.

Though she would wish him happiness, she would never be able to watch him marry someone else.

She waved goodbye to Lily and had just closed the door to the shop when she heard Lily frantically calling her name.

"Telephone," she yelled. "It's him."

Back in the office, Carolyn picked up the phone at her desk. Lily's words rang in her ears. What if he meets someone while he's back in his country? What if that was why he was calling?

But it wasn't. He only wanted to tell her he was returning at the end of the week. She heaved a sigh of relief.

"I'm glad," she said. "Because there's so much I can't do without you—for the wedding I mean. I'll pick you up at the airport," she said before she thought about it. She only thought that he might be glad to see her, as glad as she was to see him. He might kiss her again. She was so restless she went out to buy a cup of coffee instead of going to the florist. But when she got back she couldn't sit still. She paced back and forth at the window.

What would Tarik say when she reported she'd accomplished practically nothing on his sister's wedding? That she'd accomplished practically nothing period. She didn't know what was wrong with her or how she'd ever get back to normal. All she knew was she was counting the minutes until his return.

Tarik hung up the phone and went back to the massive power plant his father had built a long time ago when they first began drilling for oil in the hot desert sun. He remembered his father taking him to the construction site as a child, sitting on his father's shoulders and wearing an adult-size hard hat. How proud he'd been that his father was in charge of this massive project. How he knew even then that he was expected to fill his father's shoes one day. To fulfill his father's dream of finding a way to refine and distribute the oil from this country. Now that dream was about to be realized.

He wondered who would take over for him some day? So far there was no heir apparent to ride on his shoulders, and it didn't look as if there would be unless he did something about it. But what? After a week here, he knew he could no longer marry a woman from his country. He'd been away too long. However prominent, rich and well-connected she was, he no longer had much in common with a woman like that. For years he'd straddled two cultures, one foot in the United States and one foot in the Middle East. But now he realized he was more American than anything else. It made sense to marry an American woman. To have children with her. To carry them on his shoulders. To instill a sense of responsibility in them. To raise them. To love them.

But where and how? He had a house in San Francisco and the U.S. headquarters of the family business was there. He couldn't imagine living and working anywhere else. Other relatives would run the company from here in the desert. They didn't have the experience yet to fix problems like the one he'd just repaired, but they would.

Now that he was finished, he could go home. When exactly had America become his home? In the past he'd always thought of this country, the country of his ancestors as his home. That was no longer true. The house on the cliff in the city by the bay seemed more like home, and he was looking forward to going there. Did it have something to do with the woman who would meet him at the airport?

He couldn't deny that he'd been thinking of her often.

What would happen if he became involved with her? Wasn't it too late to ask that question? Wasn't he already involved? He had no father to warn him this time. He had only the voice inside his head to tell him to forget her. That she was wrong for him. She was emotional and romantic. Anyone with her job would be. But that voice was strangely silent about that. His head was full of images of her.

He wasn't thinking clearly. It was the heat, the blazing sun shining on his head. When he got back and got Yasmine married off he'd turn his attention to his own problems. Find someone for himself. If he expected Yasmine to marry out of a sense of duty, to someone of wealth and power, to expand the family's fortune, he must expect the same from himself. That night he called Meera to tell her when he was returning.

"Any word from Yasmine?" he asked her. He'd left messages for her and told her to call him.

"Nothing," she said. "Shall I send a taxi to fetch you at the airport?"

"No, I have a ride. What else has happened there?"

"That cat has been scratching the patio furniture," she said dourly.

"He's only a cat," he said. "We'll have it refinished. Has Mavis come by to see the cat?"

"Oh yes, every day. I watch her from the window."

He wanted to ask if Carolyn ever came with her mother. But of course she didn't. She had other things to do.

"If Yasmine calls, tell her I must speak to her. It's urgent. We don't have much time left now."

"Are you sure she'll come?" Meera asked.

What a question. Of course she would come. But deep down inside he was riddled with doubts. And thoughts that began with What if...

What if she refused to marry Jeffrey?

What if she never got on the plane and she stayed in Switzerland?

What if the whole thing fell apart?

No, it couldn't happen. It was too important. It meant too much. However stubborn she was, she wouldn't ruin their father's plans for the company. She knew as well as he did how important it was to make his dreams come true. To finish what he had started.

"Don't worry," he said. "Of course she'll come."

Chapter Eight

He was much too happy to see Carolyn for his own good. He felt light-headed and slightly dizzy. Of course that could be due to the long flight. Even in first class it was a long time to be cooped up in a plane. He'd thought about her nonstop, but he wasn't prepared for the real thing. She looked more beautiful than he remembered. Her auburn hair tumbled over her shoulders. Her face glowed. He intended to shake her hand, but when they met, he dropped his briefcase and swept her into his arms. Lord, how he'd missed her. Missed having someone to talk to.

She drove and they talked on the way to his house. He told her about the problems he'd faced and what he'd done to solve them. She didn't understand the technicalities, but she listened, sympathized and asked questions. She told him what progress she'd made on the wedding. The most important thing on her agenda was the selection of the dress. And after that the band, the rings, the photographer...the list seemed endless.

"You're well-organized. You have everything under control," he said watching her maneuver her small car out of the airport.

"Well, not quite everything," she said modestly.

"No, there is Yasmine," he said soberly. "You can't control her." Neither could he. Neither could anyone. He had to rely on his sister's sense of obligation and her family loyalty.

Carolyn turned to look at him, raising her eyebrows inquisitively. "Have you heard something?"

He shook his head. "That's the problem. I've heard nothing. She doesn't return my calls."

"You said she was busy with exams."

"That's what I said, but..." He didn't finish the sentence. It didn't have an ending. Or rather it had too many possible endings. None of them bore thinking about.

"I once tried to tell you my philosophy of weddings," she said.

"And I refused to listen, didn't I? You must have thought me boorish and arrogant. Go ahead. I'm listening now. Tell me." He fixed his eyes on her profile, the outline of her chin, the curve of her cheek, the curls that brushed her shoulder and wished he could take back his behavior at their initial meeting. Yes, he'd been anxious about the wedding, but he finally realized that was no excuse to interrupt her consultation with the other couple.

"Weddings are only a reflection of life. Of the bride and the groom's lives. They're funny and sad and happy. Like life. They're full of promise and hope and even an occasional disappointment. They are about human beings. You won't believe this but they are also about emotion. And love. Which is why they can't be perfect. Things go wrong no matter what. It's best to be prepared for that. It's Murphy's Law. Do you know Murphy's Law?'' she asked.

''Anything that can go wrong, does go wrong,'' he said.

''Exactly.''

''Nothing can go wrong at this wedding,'' he said, his jaw clenched. ''There's too much at stake.''

''Believe me, things go wrong at the most perfectly planned weddings. If perfection is what you're after, you're bound to be disappointed. A wedding is a celebration of love whether you believe in it or not, with all of its ups and downs and imperfections.''

''If that's your philosophy, we're miles apart,'' he said. ''I see a wedding as the merging of two families. As a presentation to the world of two people as a couple,'' he said. ''That's my philosophy.''

''I can accept that,'' she said. ''I was just trying to prepare you. Your sister's wedding is full of possibilities for everything to go wrong. She's not here for one thing.''

''She will be,'' he said.

''All right,'' she said.

''Drop me off at my office,'' he said abruptly.

''You're going to work now?'' she asked.

He rubbed his forehead. ''I must.''

''I made an appointment at the bridal salon for ten o'clock tomorrow,'' she said.

''I'll be there,'' he said curtly. His mind was spinning. His mood was black. He hadn't slept last night, and he was suffering from jet lag. On top of that Carolyn thought things would go wrong at the wedding. Just the kind of observation he didn't need to hear right now. Her philosophy was diametrically opposed to his. He should have known and stuck to safer subjects. He got out of the car with his suitcase and briefcase and leaned down to thank her. She nodded but didn't speak. In a moment she was gone, her car had disappeared in the traffic. He stood on the curb staring blankly at the cars and buses without seeing them.

Carolyn felt as though she'd just said goodbye to a stranger. Certainly not the same man she'd picked up at the airport a short time ago. Not the same man who'd hugged her to him. Whose face was bronzed from the desert sun. Whose eyes seemed to light up when he saw her. Who made her feel like jumping for joy just to see him. Until she told him her philosophy. It wasn't that radical. It wasn't that strange. But he didn't like it. Didn't want to hear it. Because it wasn't his philosophy.

He was worried, she could tell. He was used to being in control of every situation, making things happen. Solving problems. But this wedding might be one problem he couldn't solve. Because of the human factor. She'd tried to tell him that. He didn't listen. He wouldn't listen the first night he came into her shop. And he still didn't. She'd almost fooled herself into believing he'd changed. He'd fooled her mother into thinking he was not a control freak, he was just a rich, charming, lovable man who happened to be a sheik. How she wished he was. But she knew better.

She went back to the shop determined to focus on one of her other weddings. She'd spent entirely too much time on Tarik, but it was no use thinking she could put him out of her mind. Especially with Lily around.

"So he's back," Lily said. "How did things go?"

"Things went fine where he was. He fixed the problem. It's the wedding problem he can't fix. Because there is no fix. I told him to expect the unexpected. Especially for this wedding."

Lily tossed the society section of the newspaper onto

Carolyn's desk. "It's official anyway. According to the newspaper. The bride's picture and everything."

Carolyn eagerly turned the pages. "Good. Yes, they got it all right."

"She's gorgeous," Lily said, leaning over Carolyn's shoulder. "Just like her brother."

"I just hope she's got a more flexible outlook on life," Carolyn said. "He described her as being stubborn, headstrong and spoiled."

"Uh-oh. I'm getting worried."

"Don't you get worried, too. It will all be over in two weeks. The happy couple will be off on their honeymoon and life will be back to normal. No more sheik. No more..."

"No more sheik? You mean you're not going to see him again?" Lily asked.

"No reason to," Carolyn said lightly. But inside there was a pain in the middle of her ribs. She'd been so wrong about him at times. Other times she'd been dead right. Right in her first opinion.

"I thought maybe you two..." Lily said.

"Oh, no. Didn't I tell you he was not my type?"

"Yes, but when I saw him in person he was so charming, so...so..."

"So debonair, so cosmopolitan, so distinguished.... Is that what you were going to say?" Carolyn asked.

"How did you guess?" Lily asked with a grin. "Here you are. The travel agent dropped off the tickets for you."

Carolyn reached for the manila envelope and stared at the tickets to Fiji and the connecting hop to the resort. She could see it as clearly as if she were there. The bamboo huts, the pristine white sand beaches and the aquamarine water. If the couple wasn't in love before they got to the mall island off the coast, they'd have to be in love when hey left. If not with each other, with the place. Unless they ad their hearts set on Paris or Niagara Falls.

"That's where you'd go, wouldn't you?" Lily asked, vith a nod at the envelope.

Carolyn nodded sheepishly. "I know it's not right for vedding planners to impose their own taste on their clients, ut in this case I've never even met my client. Tarik told ne to use my own judgment. So I picked my dream honeymoon spot. I've suggested it to various clients in the past, ut no one ever went for it before. I hope it's not a miske."

"Absolutely not. It's a wonderful idea. I can't imagine nyone not being happy there. I'm sure they'll thank you ome day. So don't feel guilty about imposing your taste n them."

"I won't." She sighed. "I won't feel guilty, but I might el a little envious."

"One of these days it will be your turn, Carolyn."

"Sure it will," she said glibly. "But it's time to stop ntasizing and get back to work. First I have a question r you. Where did you go on your honeymoon, Lily?" arolyn asked.

"Camping at Lake Tahoe," Lily said with a dreamy nile. "It was wonderful. We hiked all day, made a campe at night, then zipped our sleeping bags together. Oh, it s so romantic. Twenty years ago, but I'll never forget "

"That's the way it should be. A honeymoon that sets the ne for your whole life. Did anything go wrong?"

"No, it was perfect except for the bear who broke into r rations and ate all our food on the second day out."

"See what I mean? Life is full of the unexpected. Exactly what I was trying to tell Tarik. He's determined that this wedding go off without a hitch. You and I know it's impossible."

"We also know that love conquers all," Lily said. "It can withstand a disastrous wedding and a problematic honeymoon. So we do our job, then sit back and wish Tarik's sister and her husband every happiness. As for you, my dear partner, I'm certain you'll find the man of your dreams, and you'll be planning your own wedding and honeymoon one of these days."

"Will I?" Carolyn asked wistfully.

Lily nodded emphatically and Carolyn forced herself to put the plane tickets in her top drawer and stop daydreaming. Maybe it was time to move to Alaska or get a differen job after all. Because of all the weddings she'd planned this was the most difficult. Not because the bride wasn' here, not because of the short notice. It was because thi wedding brought out all her secret longings and wishes. B throwing herself so intensely into the preparations, it wa almost as if it was her wedding she was planning. But wasn't. Envy was a terrible thing and for the first time i her career, she envied the bride. Indulging in fantasy wa almost as bad. Fantasizing about marrying a man wh didn't believe in love and was out of her reach anywa didn't help her find that sweet, gentle, caring man she' always dreamed about.

She promised herself that after this wedding, she'd d something about her own life and her own future. A ne job or a new location. Right now she had to concentrate the wedding at hand.

Carolyn felt apprehensive about meeting Tarik at the bridal shop the next day. What if he was still in the san black mood as the day before? What if they couldn't agr on a dress? What if they picked a dress that didn't fit and that his sister hated? How was she going to pick out a dress that she loved and have it worn by someone else without feeling a sense of loss and failure, and worse, jealousy?

The answer was obvious. It was because she was a professional. She was not here to get emotionally involved with the dress or the gifts or the wedding itself. And especially not with the bride's brother. She was here to plan the wedding and then step back and watch from the sidelines like the director of a play. If the actors flubbed their lines, if the scenery got knocked down or someone forgot a prop, that was life.

She would do her best, but when the organ started playing the wedding march she would be somewhere behind a pillar—out of sight, and out of mind. That's the way it always was and always would be for a wedding consultant. Unless it was her wedding. Then and only then would she take center stage and play the lead in her own life story. Until then she was only the stage manager.

Up until now that had been enough for her. Now she was having doubts about the job and about her life. If Tarik hadn't walked into her shop that evening, would she still feel this way? No, she'd be deep in the plans for the ceremony with the penguin rock-giving exchange, keeping an emotional distance from the job and otherwise content with her life.

Carolyn was going through the rack of dresses at the bridal shop when Tarik came up behind her. She could feel his presence before he spoke, before she turned around. It couldn't have been anyone else because he was unique. Was it because he was a sheik or was it because he was Tarik? She didn't know. She only knew he smelled of expensive European soap and rich leather. She took a deep breath and turned around. He looked better today, the lines in his forehead had faded and his smile made her feel warm inside. Warm all over. So warm she fanned her face with her hand. She returned his smile and willed her heart to stop thumping with excitement.

"I'm sorry to be late," he said. He had manners like his clothes, impeccable and tailored just for him. Impossible to imagine him without them.

"That's all right." She flipped through a few dresses just to have something to do besides stare at him. How silly to be nervous around him. To find herself with a case of pre-wedding jitters. He was not her groom and she was not getting married. "I...uh...I'm not sure exactly what type of dress we're looking for. Are you?" she asked Tarik.

The clerk pulled out a dress inspired by Princess Diana's with puffed sleeves and a matching tiara. "This is very romantic," she said to Tarik.

He shrugged. "What do you think?" he asked Carolyn.

"Perhaps a little too..."

"Yes, I think so, too," he said, catching her meaning.

The clerk showed them another dress of ivory lace trimmed with pearls. "Classic," she said.

Another shrug. They were getting nowhere fast.

The next was a *peau de soie* column with narrow straps and a long veil. After that a tulle gown with an embroidered bodice. Tarik looked dazed.

"I'll try them all on," she told the clerk. "Maybe that will make a difference."

Tarik nodded. "I'm sure they'll look better on you than on the hanger," he said.

"Thank you, I think," Carolyn said.

The clerk smiled benevolently at him.

"Quite a romantic, your man," she murmured as she hung the dresses in the dressing room. Instead of going to the trouble of denying he was hers, Carolyn just nodded. It was all too complicated.

"It's clear he adores you," she added.

Carolyn almost choked. She must say that to all the cus- tomers. Because it wasn't clear to her at all. He respected ner, which was quite a lot considering how he'd felt about ner a short time ago. And sometimes she thought there was nore than that. There was an attraction between them that oth were fighting off. There were those kisses and the lectricity in the air. Surely she wasn't the only one who elt it.

The first dress she modeled was an A-line satin with a lrop-waist. The skirt billowed to the floor, the train trailing ehind as Carolyn walked out into the showroom. Tarik vas seated in a leather chair watching her. She walked lowly, feeling his eyes on her, on her bare shoulders, her ips and lingering on her breasts. It was nothing personal, he told herself. He was looking at the dress, not at her. here was no need to feel like she was spiking a fever of ne hundred and five.

"What do you think?" she asked. Maybe he'd like the rst one. It wouldn't be her first choice, but there was noth- g wrong with it. Then another task could be crossed off er list. They could wrap up the dress and leave without rther ado. She could go back to work and stop partici- ating in this charade. So could he.

She turned around so he could see the train. She couldn't e him, but she felt his gaze traveling over her body. oose bumps popped out on her arms although it was warm the shop. Very warm. She turned to face him. He shook s head. "Isn't it a little too ruffled, too..."

"Frilly?"

"Yes."

She went back in the dressing room. "Something simpler," she said to the clerk.

"He has a mind of his own," the clerk said unzipping the dress from the back.

"Oh, yes," Carolyn agreed. That he did. The clerk took a charmeuse slip dress in the style of Carolyn Bessette Kennedy's wedding dress off the hanger and lifted it over he head.

"Ooooh," the clerk said. "Simple, yet elegant. That' your style. Here, let me adjust those straps."

Carolyn went out to show Tarik. From the look on hi face and the hushed silence she thought this might be th one. He cocked his head to one side and contemplated th dress until she thought she might faint from exhaustion Finally he shook his head.

"Let's see some more," he said.

She sighed and went back to the dressing room.

Tarik listened to the murmur of the voices in the dressin room. He crossed one leg over the other and settled int the chair. What a way to spend a morning. While pape piled up on his desk, while lawyers waited to see him, h was watching a fashion show. But what a show. He'd like every dress Carolyn had tried on. But it wasn't the dress he liked. It was her. But he decided to play it cool. Or th show would be over after the first dress. And he didn't wa that to happen.

How could he ever choose? Carolyn looked sensation in everything she wore. Even running shorts. She was goi to make a beautiful bride one day. He hated to think of h marrying, but she would. Even though she said she didr meet any eligible men. One of these days she would. He hoped he wouldn't be around then because just the thought filled him with an envy for the unknown groom. Envy was a trait unbecoming of a sheik.

She was back in yet another dress, the creamy white satin décolletage blending with her creamy white skin. He took a deep breath and told himself to be objective. Focus on the task of choosing the dress. At the same time as long as he was closeted in the small shop he could give his mind a rest from the anxiety over the wedding and the merger. Even though he'd always denied he was prone to any kind of emotional problems or detours into fantasy, he had to admit he'd changed.

It must be the upcoming wedding that changed him because right now he was feeling just as susceptible to these weaknesses as the next person. Watching Carolyn try on wedding dresses made him feel like he was about to take a giant step off the deep end of a long pier. His heart banged against his ribs at the thought of jumping into unknown waters. Taking a chance. Hopefully, when the wedding was over he'd revert to his normal sane and sensible self. But right now, for example, it would be so easy to fantasize that this wedding was his. Carolyn was his bride, and he was going to claim her for his own in a classic, high-ceilinged cathedral. He'd kiss the bride the way he had during the run-through, only this time they'd live happily ever after.

If she were getting married she'd be wearing one of these magnificent dresses and her veil would cover her face as she came down the aisle toward him. At the last minute he'd lift the veil and he'd see her smile up at him. See her eyes glow and hear her promise to love, honor and… That was the problem. He couldn't promise to love her, and she would never promise to obey him. That was crucial to his and any sheik's happiness. His father had warned him over and over. His father was right.

No matter how much he liked these dresses, and every one looked beautiful on her, he decided to find some flaw with each of them or the fashion show would be over. Carolyn would change back into her slacks and blazer and go back to work. They'd both be jarred into reality. A place he didn't want to return to. Not yet.

The clerk came out of the dressing room. He was glad to see she didn't appear to be getting impatient. She shouldn't for the money he intended to spend on this dress

"The next dress is an embroidered mother-of-pear sleeveless top and a tulle gown with a ballerina skirt," she said. "Your fiancée looks lovely in it."

"I'm sure she does," he said, not bothering to tell he Carolyn wasn't his fiancée. Then he'd have to launch int a discussion about his sister and try to explain why sh wasn't there, when he was beginning to wonder himsel The clerk knew he knew nothing about tulle or mother-of pearl. But he knew one thing—Carolyn would look stun ning in it.

"She's going to be a beautiful bride," the woman said

Tarik frowned. Of course she would. That went withou saying. It was just what he feared. She'd be a beautif bride. Some day. But not his bride. She did look gorgeou in the ballerina skirt, but he shook his head. He hoped the weren't running out of dresses. He wanted to see mor More dresses. More of Carolyn.

The next time she came out it was in a hand-beade chiffon gown. The clerk described it as sexy and a trif naughty. Tarik drew in a quick breath when he saw Caroly in it. It clung to her body, to her breasts and hips until it flared out halfway to the floor.

"How do you like it?" Tarik asked Carolyn, his eyes glued to the narrow straps, wondering how they managed to hold the gown up and what would happen if they didn't.

"I feel like a siren," she said with a little smile that could only be described as sexy and as naughty as the dress itself. "Would Yasmine like it?" she asked.

He didn't know. Yasmine was the furthest thing from his mind. He couldn't tear his eyes off of Carolyn. He wanted to say it was not a dress for a virgin. But he didn't trust his voice, so he merely shrugged. She went back in the dressing room. He didn't know if she was disappointed at his reaction or not. He only knew he wanted to hold the picture of her smile in his head. Even if it wasn't for him.

It was a long time before she came out again. So long, Tarik rested his head on the back of the chair and stretched his legs out. Strange how he wasn't impatient. Totally unlike him. He felt he'd left the old Tarik back in the office and a different man was devoting a morning to looking at wedding dresses. Who was he kidding? He was not there to look at dresses. He was there to look at Carolyn.

When she finally came out she was wearing a white-faille taffeta with an embroidered ruffle. Her hair was pinned up on top of her head with rich auburn tendrils trailing down her neck. While he watched she slowly pulled on a pair of above-the-elbow white gloves. It was such a natural gesture, but the way she did it sent a bolt of pure desire shooting through him. He shifted his position. Tried to tear his eyes away from her, but he couldn't. Their eyes met and held for an eternity. The clerk was rattling on about the well-known designer but Tarik wasn't listening.

He finally broke the spell, tore his gaze away and sat up

straight. He tuned out the clerk's voice so he could concentrate on the way the ruffle lined the top of the bodice, gazing at the outline of Carolyn's breasts. Yes, this was the dress for her. He could imagine her getting married in this dress. In those gloves. She held her head high, her shoulders straight, as if she too could imagine it. He knew she felt good in the dress. As good as she looked, which was spectacular.

"We'll take it," he said.

"What?" Carolyn looked startled. As if she'd been in a daze.

"You like it, don't you?" he asked.

"Yes, but..."

"Then we'll take it."

"You didn't ask how much it was," she said.

"It doesn't matter."

"What about your sister, will she like it?"

"Of course. Just as she'll like the silverware, the dishes, the church, and the hotel reception. She's very easy to please." He hoped God would forgive him for that white lie. Yasmine was not easy to please. Unless she'd changed. He could only hope.

"Just one question," the clerk said, turning to Tarik. "How formally will you be dressed? Just so we have some idea."

"Me? Not that it matters, but I'll wear the traditional white headdress, which was my father's. In fact I have it in the car to take it to the cleaner now."

"I've never seen one," the clerk said.

"I'll bring it in," he offered.

When he returned from the car and tried the formal attire on, it made him feel different wearing the white cloth tied with gold cord, older and more serious. Carolyn's eyes wid ened and she stared long and hard at him. He didn't know what she was thinking.

"Next is the ring," he said, when she'd changed back into her street clothes and he'd taken off his royal headdress. He hadn't intended to go ring shopping, but he didn't want to go back to the office.

Her eyes widened in surprise.

"Didn't I tell you? We have to pick out the ring for the groom."

"I'm afraid I..."

"It shouldn't take that long," he said, steering her to his car with his hand on the small of her back. "Just a plain gold band is customary, right?"

She nodded and then he said they couldn't look at rings on an empty stomach. Though she protested, he insisted on driving through a drive-through at a fast-food restaurant, ordering a cheeseburger deluxe for both of them and eating it in the car on the way to the jewelers.

"I didn't ask," he said. "Was there somewhere else you'd rather go?"

"No, I just thought you'd be going straight back to work."

"I probably should," he said. "But my work is to see that this wedding comes off. If I'm not mistaken, that's your work, too. And we can't do our work if we're weak from hunger. Trying on dresses must be hard work. Which one did you like the best? Be honest."

"The one you bought. It was simple and elegant. I just hope your sister feels the same."

"She will. And if she doesn't, the wedding will be over before she realizes it."

"What will you do with the dress?"

"I don't know. Donate it to charity, perhaps," he said.

He drove and ate at the same time. She nibbled on a French fry. "Is this something else you've never had before?" she asked, looking amused at his obvious enjoyment as he reached into a bag for a soft drink.

"When I first came here to the university I ate many hamburgers until we got our apartment and our cook. I always enjoyed them immensely. But since then, it sounds funny, I know, but I haven't had time for your fast food. But I realized today it takes hardly any time at all which works out well for this afternoon. Most days I usually work right through lunch, or I have to host a business lunch at Jacks or some other restaurant where the waiters wear black ties and no one pays attention to the food because they're talking business.

"I appreciate your coming with me today," he continued. "One, because I hate to eat alone, and two, because it wouldn't hurt you to put on a few pounds. I noticed in the bridal shop that many of the gowns were a little large on you."

"Since I'm not getting married, it really doesn't matter," she said. "I don't think anyone has ever said I'm too thin, except maybe my mother."

"Next time I'll take you to a decent restaurant. I owe it to you."

"That's not necessary," she said.

"Not for you, but for me. I was brought up to reciprocate. And to pay my debts," he said.

"You may owe my mother, but you don't owe me," she said.

The argument ended when they reached the jewelry store. There was a security guard at the door and deep carpets inside with a few well-dressed, soft-spoken customers conversing with clerks.

Of course the clerk also thought they were the newly-weds-to-be. He brought out ring after ring until Tarik finally chose one.

"Excellent choice," the clerk enthused. "Why don't you put it on his finger?" he asked Carolyn. "Just as you'll do during the ceremony."

"No, I...all right," Carolyn said.

Tarik smiled at her to show he understood. Why bother to correct people when the truth was so complicated?

She grasped his hand and pushed the ring on. He looked into her eyes and the words ran through his mind as they must have run through hers.

With this ring I thee wed.

Tarik stared at the ring, at their two hands together, wondering if some day it would be his turn, his ring, his wedding, his bride....

Now that he had Tarik fitted, the clerk shifted his attention to Carolyn and did a double take when he noticed Carolyn wasn't wearing a ring at all. He almost rubbed his hands with glee.

"I have just the ring for you," he said, opening a glass case with a small key. He brought out a stunning diamond solitaire and slipped it on her finger before either one of them could stop him with the usual story about how it wasn't their wedding, they were just standing in for others. The story that never seemed to get past their lips.

Carolyn gasped as if the brilliance hurt her eyes.

"It's beautiful," Tarik said.

The clerk beamed and before Carolyn could take it off he'd found a platinum band studded with tiny diamonds to go with it. He handed it to Tarik and told him to put it on her.

"Now it's your turn," he said.

Tarik knew he should protest. He should set the man

straight immediately before he got any more ideas, but he didn't. For some reason he just slipped the ring onto Carolyn's finger so that it nested there next to the solitaire.

"You see?" the clerk said. "It's perfect for her."

"Yes, it is," Tarik said, admiring her slim tapered fingers. She was meant to wear diamonds. He wished he could buy them for her. Of course he could, but she probably wouldn't accept them. She would barely accept a lunch invitation, let alone precious jewelry. He turned back to the clerk. "We're not in the market for..."

"A wedding ring lasts forever," the clerk said. "It's the most important purchase you'll ever make."

"Yes, of course," Tarik said. Impulsively he took Carolyn's hand and held it up so he could admire the sparkle of the diamonds. Her fingers were cool. Was it his imagination or did she smell like the roses she'd suggested for the bridal bouquet? Was he getting too close to this wedding? Or just too close to the wedding consultant?

As if they'd rehearsed, both he and Carolyn took their rings off at the same time, quickly as if they were burning holes in their fingers, and laid them on the counter. Tarik whipped out his credit card and bought the plain gold band for his sister's groom. He told the clerk they weren't going to buy the diamonds. The poor man looked as unhappy if they'd told him they weren't getting married at all. At least Tarik spared him the truth.

He put the ring into his pocket and drove her back to the bridal shop.

"Dress. Ring," he said before she got out of the car "What is next?"

"Music. The band," she said. "I meant to tell you there's a band you might like that is playing at a fund raiser on Saturday evening. We can drop by and see wha you think of them. I know they're available, but I don't know if you'll like them."

"Yes, a good idea. Only my cousins are arriving early for the wedding on Saturday to stay with me. They're twins, young swinging bachelors and I promised to take them out on the town. I'm afraid I'm out of touch with that lifestyle. I was hoping you could make some suggestions."

"You thought I would know where to take them?" she asked incredulously.

"You know everything," he said. "Or if you don't know, you know how to find out."

"I guess I can find out. I assume you mean the club scene. All I know is that the action is definitely in the Soma area, but I'll have to get the names of the places to go. I guess that means you'll be tied up on Saturday night."

"Both me and you. I assumed we could do both the fund-raiser and the clubs in one evening. The boys are presentable and will blend in with whatever crowd they run into, I assure you, so buy enough tickets for all of us and put it on my bill. The boys will certainly have an opinion on the band and the music, which might be helpful."

"Yes, sure, but..." She looked dubious. "When you say *we* do both the clubs and the party, who exactly do you mean?"

"You and I of course," he said. In two weeks, after the wedding, he'd never see her again. In the meantime he intended to see her as often as possible. Even if he had to invent excuses. Oh, the cousins were real, alright. But they hadn't asked to be taken to the clubs. They were club types, however, and he was sure they'd appreciate it.

He was infatuated with her. He admitted it. He loved the sound of her voice, the lilt of her smile, her lips, her eyes...everything about her. In two weeks she'd be out of his life forever. But until then...

Chapter Nine

Tarik had neglected to mention to Carolyn that his cousins were twins and full of the devil. They were almost as handsome as Tarik with their dark hair, and their sun-bronzed skin. Their youthful zest for life showed in their gleaming coal-black eyes.

"Where have you been keeping this beautiful lady?" Jared asked Tarik the minute he met Carolyn on Saturday evening.

Before Tarik had a chance to answer, his twin brother pressed his lips to Carolyn's hand and said he was enchanted to meet her.

Carolyn gulped in surprise then broke into a smile. She told Tarik later at the party at the San Francisco Yacht Club that they made her feel young again.

"You *are* young," he said, sitting next to her at a small candlelit table at the edge of the dance floor. He shot an appreciative glance in her direction. She was glad she'd worn a forest green dress and matching jacket that Lily said brought out the green in her eyes. Afterwards, if they did go to the clubs, she could take off the jacket and reveal thin straps and bare shoulders. Of course she could simply tell them where the clubs were and go home early. But in the festive atmosphere of a charity event that she hadn't planned and wasn't responsible for, she was able to relax and enjoy herself as she seldom did at these affairs. So much so she'd almost forgotten why they were there.

"What do you think of them?" Tarik asked leaning forward, his lips brushing her ear.

"What?" She shivered, his breath causing a shimmer to move up her spine. He looked so stunning tonight, in his dark suit and white shirt she couldn't keep her eyes off him. "Oh, they're adorable. Were you like them when you were young?"

"I meant the band," he said.

"So far so good. They seem to have a large repertoire."

"As for the boys, I was much more serious than they are. They're ladies' men, a different girl every day of the week. Maybe I should have been more like they are. Maybe I should have kicked up my heels a bit as they're doing. They'll have nothing to regret."

"Do you have something to regret?"

"Doesn't everyone?" he asked lightly. "Let's dance." He stood and extended his hand. "It's the only way to judge the band, isn't it, by dancing to their music?"

She had to agree, but she knew she should say no. She was having enough trouble resisting Tarik's charms without letting him put his arms around her and hold her close. Or she could wait for a fast dance in order to avoid any intimate physical contact. But she didn't. She let him lead her to the dance floor. She should have known he'd be a great dancer.

"Just part of a sheik's upbringing," he said when she complimented him. "Along with archery, falconry, etiquette, sailing, business. Oh, Carolyn..." He pulled her close as his voice drifted off. This was no time to talk. This was time to move with the music. To give in and let her body mold itself to his, to feel the hard muscles of his chest, his thighs, to drink in the essence of the man. To let herself forget he could never love anyone.

She had to remind herself of this every other minute Because otherwise she might be tempted to fall in love with him herself. She never thought she'd say it, but somewhere along the line, maybe it was in the church, or maybe at he mother's house when they were looking at photographs, o maybe it was in the jewelry store, she'd come to realize h wasn't what she'd first thought. She remembered telling he mother, or was it Lily, that no one would marry him.

Now she realized there'd be many women who woul want to marry him. Why hadn't they? Because he wasn' looking. Like her, he didn't meet eligible, prospectiv spouses in his line of work. There weren't many women i the oil business. Or men in the bridal business.

If she had to write him a recommendation, she'd say th sheik was chivalrous in a way few other men were. Holdin doors open, escorting her to her car, expressing concern f her safety. He was also exotic and fascinating as only foreigner can be and yet familiar from having studied i this country. Kind and thoughtful—witness his treatment her mother and her mother's cat. And most of all stron and virile. He was a take-charge man, no question abo that. What woman wouldn't want such a man? Wh woman wouldn't fall in love with him?

A woman like her, of course, who was looking for kind, gentle man who never gave orders, the complete o posite of her father. But other than her, if he let himself, he could have a line of women begging him to marry them. Just one drawback, she couldn't expect to be loved. Because Tarik didn't believe in love. So it would have to be someone content with respect, admiration and loyalty. Was that enough? Not for her.

She no longer believed he was a control freak like her father. Her mother was right about that. As head of the family, Tarik had many responsibilities both personal and financial. His father had left him in charge of a huge business and a family with many threads left untied. If he seemed demanding, it was because he had so many people depending on him. A whole country, in fact.

The music surrounded her, seeped into her pores. She could have danced all night with him. His arms around her. Swaying to the music, feeling his heartbeat through his tai-ored jacket. But the twins had other ideas. First it was ared who tapped Tarik on the shoulder and cut in.

"Where have you been all my life?" he asked Carolyn, is dark eyes dancing with fun.

Carolyn shook her head in mock dismay. "Where did ou learn such good English?" she asked.

"Boarding school in Boston," he said.

"Did they teach you to flirt, too?"

"They didn't need to. I was born to flirt. Why don't you ump that cousin of mine? We could have a great time ogether."

"I'm sure we could," she said agreeably, "but you've ot the wrong idea. Your cousin and I are just, uh...doing usiness together. I thought he explained that."

"He didn't explain why he looks at you like he wants eat you up. Why he's watching us dance with a fierce ok on his face like he wants to bash my head in."

"Come on, Jared," she said. "You're exaggerating."

"Am I?" He twirled her around so she could face Tarik, and she had to admit he didn't look happy. He was staring at her with a frown on his face. "Why don't you get rid of him and fly away with me to my villa on the Riviera?"

"*Do* you have a villa on the Riviera?" she asked.

"The family does," he said with an offhand shrug. "You'll get to meet most of them this week. My parents and some more cousins. There will be a full house at Tarik's as we gather for the wedding. So what do you say? Dump Tarik and take up with me, his swinging cousin." He gave her a conspiratorial wink.

"I say I can't dump someone I don't have," she said sternly.

The song ended, some wild, fast music started and Rahman cut in on his brother. "We thought Tarik would never find anybody like you," he said as he threw himself into the dance, waving his arms and shaking his hips. "Wait till the rest of the family sees you," he said with a grin. "They'll be impressed, in fact they'll...how do you say...totally flip out. Good thing Uncle isn't here. Or the same thing would happen as happened last time."

"I don't know what you're talking about," she said breathlessly. "You and your brother have got it all wrong. I'm not involved with your cousin. I'm just..."

"Planning Yasmine's wedding, I know, but I saw you dancing together a few minutes ago. Were you planning her wedding then, or were you planning your own?"

Carolyn's face flamed. She blamed it on the dance. "Neither. I thought we explained. We're here to check out the band. What do you think of them by the way?" Carolyn asked, carefully changing the subject.

"Not bad," he said. "So you have no interest in m

cousin, is that what you're saying? Why not, what's wrong?''

''Nothing. I like him very much,'' she said.

''Then go for it,'' he said. ''From what I can see I'd say it's mutual. I'd say Tarik has got it bad. From the minute we got off the plane, he started talking about you. Carolyn said this and Carolyn did that. I said to my brother, 'we've got to see this lady.' Now that we've seen you, we're giving you a thumbs-up,'' he said, jerking his thumb in the air. ''Uh-oh, here he comes. I'd better watch out. He looks mad.''

Tarik did indeed look mad. He scowled at his cousin who was still holding his thumb in the air. ''What was that all about?'' he asked Carolyn with a glance over his shoulder at his departing cousin.

''Oh, you know, they're kicking up their heels, just as you said. Being boys on holiday, they're a little crazy.''

''They've been in and out of trouble all their lives. Nothing serious, but what one doesn't think of, the other does. I hope they haven't bothered you with their nonsense.''

''Not at all. They're very amusing.''

''Amusing,'' he repeated, but he didn't look amused. The music swelled and he didn't say anything. She sighed, so glad to be back in his arms. She wanted the music to go on forever. She settled into his arms as if she'd never left and never wanted to. When the dance was finally over, she was afraid she wouldn't be able to walk back to their table. Her knees were weak and her head felt like it was floating above her body.

''Okay?'' he murmured, his hands on her shoulders, his dark eyes locked onto her green eyes.

She nodded. ''We'd better go. I think we've heard enough to decide on the band. Did you like them?''

"I liked the dancing," he said. "I could stay here forever with you in my arms. I never want to let you go. But I must," he said dropping his arms to his sides. "You tempt me, Carolyn."

She swallowed hard, barely conscious that the band was taking a break and they were alone on the dance floor. "How? I don't mean to."

"By just being yourself. You make me want what I can't have."

She didn't say anything, but the words circled around in her brain. *But why? Why can't you have it?* Maybe some day she'd finally hear the whole story of Tarik's life. Of what had made him distrust his feelings and refuse to believe in love. Of what his father had done.

He shook his head slowly as if he'd heard her question. Maybe he'd seen the questions in her eyes. "It's a long story and not a very interesting one. I promised the boys we'd take them to the clubs. First I must speak to the band leader and give him a retainer fee."

She mentally checked off another item on the list. Another job done. The band was set. That's what they were here for and they'd accomplished it. No reason to feel let down because Tarik refused to confide in her. If that was why she'd come tonight, she was a fool. Because it wasn't going to happen. They drove the boys to the dance club and Tarik told them to take a taxi home.

"I hope you don't mind," he said to Carolyn after his cousins had piled out of the car headed for a very swinging club, judging by the noise coming from the open door. "I'm in no mood to be jostled by crowds of leather-jacketed, bleached-hair revelers where the music is so loud we can't talk."

"Are we going to talk?" she asked hopefully.

"I think I owe it to you," he said.

But he didn't talk at all until he reached her house. He parked on the street and looked up at the one window in her apartment with the light on.

"Would you like to come up?" she asked after a long silence.

He nodded and got out of the car so he could open the door for her.

Once inside the apartment, Carolyn made coffee and kicked off her shoes. She wished he'd do the same. How could anyone relax in dress shoes and a suit and tie? But Tarik wasn't just anyone. He looked as comfortable in dress clothes as he did in running shorts. At least he settled back in her overstuffed chair and put his feet on the leather ottoman.

Carolyn turned the lights low, curled up on the couch with her bare feet tucked under her and waited. She had so many questions on her mind, but she didn't dare ask, not until Tarik was ready to answer them. He looked so serious, sipping his coffee, she was afraid of what he was going to say. She thought she was prepared. But how can anyone prepare for someone else's story?

"I've spoken to you of my father," he began.

"Yes and I've seen his portrait. He looks like a remarkable man."

"He was. I grew up wanting to please him, to be like him in every way. He often took me with him to his office and to the oil fields. I always pictured myself following in his footsteps. That was always his plan. He instilled in me a sense of pride and responsibility, both to my family and to my country."

"Which you have," she said.

"In many ways, yes," he said. "With the merger I think

I can finally say he would be proud of me. In so many ways it's the most important thing I've ever done. Which is why your help has been so invaluable.''

''Any wedding consultant could have done what I've done,'' she said modestly, looking down into her coffee cup.

''I don't think so. I don't believe any other wedding consultant would have worked so hard, given up her weekends, evenings...no, I don't know what led me to your shop that evening, but I thank God for sending you to me.''

His voice was so rich and full of meaning Carolyn felt tears spring to her eyes. She was touched by his compliments because she knew he didn't hand them out indiscriminately. She tried to smile, but her lips trembled so much she gave up.

''Back to my father,'' he said. ''I went to the university in this country as you know. It was the best place to study management. Naturally he was worried I would be corrupted by what he considered a certain moral laxity in this country, but I persuaded him by quoting his favorite proverb—The branch doesn't fall far from the tree.''

Carolyn nodded encouragingly and he continued.

''But in a way I did fall far from the tree. I fell in love I know. I said I didn't believe in love, but I did then. Sh was a girl in my history class, bright and beautiful. Whe my father came to visit, he met her and seeing how infat uated I was with her, and how serious I was abou her...which I was...he told me that marriages of the hear are not for men with vast wealth and power and respons bility. My parents' marriage was arranged by their familie and I must say it was very successful. She was a dutif wife...I know you won't like that word dutiful...but th is the truth. More than that they had a mutual respect and affection for each other."

"So you broke it off with your girlfriend?" Carolyn asked. Did that explain why he had never fallen in love again or why he didn't believe in love?

"No, I didn't. I was young and headstrong and stubborn. And feeling very independent here in this country. I told my father it was my life and my decision. He didn't protest. But I'll never forget the look on his face. There was disappointment there and sadness. He nodded and said he hoped I knew what I was doing. Of course I didn't. I was young and full of myself. I was convinced this girl was the one for me. Even though looking back we didn't have much in common. She was not a serious student and I was. I knew I only had four years to soak in as much knowledge as I could, she looked at college as a way to experience as much fun as possible."

"But you said this evening you should have kicked up your heels more," she reminded him.

"Perhaps I should. Knowing that so much responsibility was waiting for me in the future, that was my big chance, my only chance. But given my personality, perhaps I never would have, no matter how tempted I was."

Carolyn wanted to throw her arms around him, to tell him it wasn't too late. To tell him there was still time to enjoy life, to live and love again. If only he would believe in love. She wanted to smooth his furrowed brow, to kiss away his regrets, to make him forget this girl...but she didn't. What made her think she could? She gripped the edge of the couch cushion and stayed where she was.

"What happened?" she asked.

"She found someone else," he said briefly. "She went the Bahamas on spring break our senior year and met a boy there who she said was more fun than I was. I don't doubt it. I was writing my senior thesis on the disparity between oil prices and production in the developing coun- tries, and I wasn't much fun at all. But I thought...we'c come to an agreement.... She said she loved me, she wor my ring..." He shrugged as if it didn't matter. But hi expression was bleak. She knew that even if it didn't matte now, it mattered very much at the time. "In any case it al worked out for the best as you can see."

She couldn't see it at that moment. Not from the way h looked. So downcast. So lost.

"Is this the reason you don't believe in love?" sh asked.

"That may have something to do with it," he sai "Would you?"

"I...I don't know."

"Give me some evidence that love exists," he sai meeting her gaze. He looked half hopeful that she cou and half certain that she couldn't.

Her mind spun around in circles. How could she ev convince him when he didn't want to be convinced? "Wh about poetry? Could anyone who wasn't in love have wri ten 'How do I love thee, let me count the ways...' or th classic love songs like 'Endless Love'?"

"Is that the best you can do?" he asked. "Come up wi poetry and love songs? Those are cruel travesties, writt to make money for the composers, to mislead innocent pe ple into thinking they are in love."

"Don't you think you're being too pessimistic?" s asked.

"No. I think I'm being realistic."

"Then I'm sorry for you," she said sadly.

"And I'm sorry for you if you're waiting for someone to fall in love with you."

"No, I'm not," she hotly. "I'm waiting to fall in love with someone because I believe 'the love you make is equal to the love you take.'"

"Another song," he said with a half smile. "A nice one at that."

"But I haven't convinced you," she said.

"I want to tell you something," he said. "If I did fall in love, it would be with someone like you. Carolyn, you're everything I admire in a woman. Everything I want. Would you consider marrying someone who didn't love you?" His voice was low, there was no mistaking the meaning of the words.

"I...I don't know,' she stammered. But she did know. She knew after planning so many weddings that a marriage couldn't survive with only one partner in love.

"Never mind. I knew what you would say. But there are things I must tell you. Because I can't keep them to myself any longer," he said urgently. The words spilled out as if he couldn't hold them back. "You're beautiful, kind, thoughtful and sweet. That chemistry I talked about, those symptoms I made little of—the pulse speeding up, the heart pounding, all those reasons to head straight for the emergency room—I confess I'm a victim." He spread his palms out, face up, as if he was giving in to the symptoms, but Carolyn knew he wasn't. He felt them, but he dismissed them at the same time. "Tell me I'm not the only one who feels this way. Tell me you feel the same," he said, his eyes glowing like hot coals in the semi-darkened room.

"Yes of course I feel that way," she said, trying to sound matter-of-fact. "There's a certain attraction between us. Call it electricity if you want. At least we can agree it isn't love.'' The last thing she wanted to do was to confess her real feelings to Tarik. She crossed her fingers, keeping her hand out of sight in the depths of the couch. How could she say it wasn't love? If it wasn't, she didn't know what was. All she knew was that she wanted to make him happy. Help him achieve his goal, to fulfill his father's dream. And to achieve his own dreams. Was that love? If it wasn't, it would have to do until the real thing came along.

''Thank you for telling me this,'' she said. All of a sudden she was exhausted. Tired of listening, tired of talking, tired of working on a wedding that wasn't hers. Every muscle ached, every bone cried out for a respite. She was afraid she'd never even make it to her bedroom and would fall asleep on the couch.

''I'm sorry if I've bored you,'' he said, getting to his feet. He reached for her hands and pulled her up. She laced her hands behind his neck and clung to him.

''I'm not bored,'' she whispered. ''I'm sorry. Sorry I can't convince you, sorry you had such a bad experience. Sorry...''

Sorry you can't fall in love with me. Sorry I can't tell you how I feel about you without sending you running for cover. But that's just the way it has to be.

He cut off her thoughts by kissing her. All her fatigue vanished in a moment. The energy flowed through her as if she'd had an injection of a powerful stimulant, instead of just a cup of coffee. She had. It was Tarik. It was his body pressed against hers. It was his voice in her ear whispering her name. His hands framed her face and she thought she'd drown in the depths of those black eyes. But instead of feeling lost, she felt like she'd been found. With one finger he traced the outline of her cheek, and she thought she'd faint. Gentleness and strength in that one movement

The two qualities that were the sum of the man. The man she'd fallen in love with.

Slowly, carefully, he kissed her again. She kissed him back. She felt like she'd never get enough of him. That she could plumb the depths of his soul and never reach the bottom. She stumbled back against the couch, and he caught her just in time. She could smell the warmth of his skin, the coffee on his breath, the familiar smells of her own house surrounding her. He ran his hands down the sides of her arms. Every nerve ending went on alert. This is it, she thought. This is the man I've been saving myself for. The one man in the world I want more than anything, and he doesn't want me. Doesn't love me. Can't love me.

She tried to keep those thoughts in her mind, but his kisses blotted them out. Deeper and faster and more frantic they came. As if this was their last chance. Their only chance. Her whole body was on fire. No way to put it out. She didn't want to put it out. She wanted to burn until he caught fire, too, and they went up in flames together. She could have sworn that's what was happening.

They staggered forward and then backward like two drunken sailors. They were drunk on kisses, drunk on each other. Yet the strongest drink they'd had was coffee. She closed her eyes and gave in to the power of his kisses. She knew if he stopped she'd die. Right here in her own apartment.

When he finally let her go, she didn't die, but she felt like she'd lost a part of herself, like her heart or her soul or both. He ran his hand through his disheveled hair and moved backward toward the door of her apartment "If you change your mind..." he said. "You know where to find me."

She didn't answer. What else was there to say? All she

could do was to collapse on the couch and stare into space while his words echoed through the silent room.

Would you consider marrying someone who didn't love you?

Had she just rejected an offer of marriage from the richest, most generous, handsomest man she'd ever met? Had she just made the biggest mistake of her life? Or was that a hypothetical question he'd asked?

She went to bed but she couldn't sleep. Images flashed across her brain like a speeded-up, out-of-focus home movie. Tarik running with her in the park, Tarik in his study with her mother's cat, Tarik holding her in his arms on the dance floor and Tarik flooding her mind and her senses with his kisses. She told herself she'd waited this long, she could wait a little longer for a man to fall in love with her, to love her as much as she loved him.

She groaned and covered her head with a pillow. How long should she wait? It was possible he'd never come along and if he did, he wouldn't be Tarik. She sat up straight in bed. She'd do it. Tomorrow she'd tell him. She'd tell him she *would* consider marrying someone who didn't love her. She'd do more than consider it. She'd do it. Then if he was serious, if the question was real, he'd say she'd made him the happiest man in the world. And she'd be the happiest woman.

She'd finally be planning her own wedding. Because now she knew. Just as it was impossible to have the perfect wedding, it was impossible to find the perfect mate. But with Tarik she'd come as close as she possibly could. She smiled to herself. Those voices that kept saying what about love were finally silenced, and she fell into a deep sleep.

Chapter Ten

Carolyn woke early, pulled on sweatpants and a shirt and went out for a walk on the Marina Green before work. She tried to run, but her legs wouldn't cooperate. She'd made coffee when she woke up, but when she tried to pour herself a cup, her fingers shook too much so she stuffed her hands into her pockets and walked out the door. She needed fresh air to calm her nerves. The mist rose off the bay, a cool wind blew through the Golden Gate. She inhaled deeply but it didn't help. Her heart was pounding and her mind was going round and round in circles. What would she say? What would he say?

She put it off until afternoon. She had to give herself time to think. Besides she had work to do. Bills to pay. Last minute calls about the flowers, the church, the last fitting for the dress. That she would put off as long as possible. She jumped every time the phone rang. She thought he might call, but he didn't.

Instead, her mother called and wanted her to look at an

apartment with her after work. She was getting anxious to move and reclaim her cat.

"Have you talked to him today?" her mother asked when she picked her up in her car. No need to ask who "him" was. She knew.

Carolyn shook her head.

Her mother gave her a curious glance. "I noticed a lot of excitement going on at the house when I was there to see Max. People coming and going."

"His cousins are here for the wedding. Maybe some more relatives have arrived though the wedding is a little over a week away." That was why he hadn't called. He was busy with his relatives. Of course, that was it. She tried to pay attention to the new apartment, tried to make the appropriate responses as her mother asked her what she thought about the size of the closets, about the amount of the deposit, and the condition of the kitchen floor. But her mind was elsewhere and her mother knew it.

"Worried about the wedding?" she asked. "You shouldn't be. You've done many others, and they've all turned out fine."

"Yes, but this is special," Carolyn said.

"So is he," her mother said softly.

She smiled briefly and went home to pace around her apartment and stare out the window as if she expected a visitor. But no one came. It was her own fault. All she had to do was to call him or go see him. After all, she knew where to find him. But she couldn't or wouldn't. She was too scared. Scared he'd say yes, scared he'd say no.

After a sleepless night, she went to the office, shuffled papers on her desk and finally at ten o'clock, unable to stand the suspense another minute, she drove to his house. She didn't know what she'd say or how she'd say it, she ust knew she had to go there. There were cars in the driveway, there was music coming from an upstairs window. She knocked on the front door but no one came. If they ouldn't hear the sound of her fist, surely they'd hear the ound of her heart pounding. Finally Meera appeared, wearng a dark red sari and a deep frown, her hair pulled back rom her face in a smooth knot, her face looking lined and red.

"Yes? Oh, it's you," she said.

"Good morning," Carolyn said politely. She knew from xperience that a wedding can frazzle even the steadiest erves. Meera made no move to let her pass. "May I come ?"

Meera shrugged. "Might as well. Everyone else is here."

"Everyone?"

"Including Yasmine. They're in the library, but I ouldn't go there if I were you."

Carolyn teetered back and forth in the doorway, wracked ith indecision. Yasmine, here, already? That was good, asn't it? Maybe she should wait to hear from Tarik after .

"Don't just stand there, come in," Meera said impantly, turning on her heel, obviously expecting Carolyn to llow her. "Wait in there," she said pointing to the great om. Then she disappeared.

Carolyn stood on an antique Oriental rug in the middle the room, listening to rock music coming from someere on the second story, admiring the way the light came ough the skylight and illuminated the wall hangings. om the library came the murmur of voices, first soft, now der. So loud she recognized Tarik's voice. But she ldn't make out the words.

She knew she shouldn't. She knew it was none of her

business, but her feet didn't get the message. She walked across the hall and stood next to the library door.

"You don't know what you're saying," Tarik said. His voice was tense, strained. "You're much too young to make a decision like that."

A young woman's voice answered with quiet conviction. "I'm nineteen years old and I know what I want." It was Yasmine. Carolyn raised her eyebrows and instinctively leaned against the door so she could hear better.

"If Father was here..." he said.

"But he isn't," she said. "You're here and I'm here and life goes on. This is my life we're talking about." Carolyn knew from the sound of Yasmine's voice she had much in common with her brother. Stubbornness and determination to begin with.

There was a long silence. Carolyn could picture Tarik pacing back and forth, his sister glaring at him from across the room.

"Your life, yes," he said. "But what you do with your life affects many other people."

"You, for example," she said angrily.

"Yes, me, of course. But the whole extended family is affected by what you do. Which is why, in some part, they are here to see you get married in less than two weeks."

"No."

Carolyn gasped. Maybe Tarik did, too. She couldn't tell.

"What?" he said, his voice ominously low.

"I said no. I came here to tell you I'm not going to marry someone I don't love to please my family. I don't even know the man."

"You'll get to know him."

"In one week?" she asked incredulously.

"You'll have the rest of your life. Mother and Father..."

"I know what they did. I know they never saw each other until their wedding day, and they lived happily ever after. But that was them, and this is me. I would never agree to anything like that, and I can't believe they would ask me. After all, you and I are of a different generation. We were raised differently. We were sent abroad to study. We've been exposed to other ways of life and to other people since we were small.

"The country has changed. The world has changed. I've changed. I don't expect a man to take care of me for the est of my life. Not you and not my husband. I'm going to e independent. I want to work. Everyone has changed but ou, Tarik. I'm sure even father would agree it's too late or arranged marriages."

"You're wrong. He wanted to arrange one for me."

"And..."

"And I was young and stubborn like you are. I refused," e said.

"Are you sorry you did?"

"That's beside the point," he said.

"It's exactly the point," she countered. "You wouldn't o what you're asking me to do."

"I've told you a dozen times that if the Bransons had a aughter I'd marry her in a minute and spare you whatever ain this seems to be causing you."

"And I've told you a dozen times I won't marry some-e I don't love. To you marriage is only a contract. What ould happen if you married, as you want me to do, for nvenience. Then you met and fell in love with someone se. What would you do?"

"Nothing," he said. "Yes, marriage is a contract, but a cred contract, to be kept at all costs."

"That's easy for you to say," she said, "because you

don't believe in love. Unless you've changed your mind." There was a long pause. "Have you?"

"Of course not," he said gruffly.

"I have no more to say to you, Tarik." Her voice dropped. She sounded more sad than angry. "You're my legal guardian, but you're also my brother. We're all that's left of the family. Just you and I. I thought I meant more to you than this. More than a chattel to be traded for favorable terms in a business merger. Since I'm underage you can stop me from marrying someone I love, but you can't force me to marry someone I don't love."

"You're tired, Yasmine. You've had a long trip. Go res and we'll talk some more. Wait until you hear the plan for the wedding. You'll change your mind. We've foun you a beautiful dress, and the church is magnificent."

"Return the dress and cancel the church. I never tol you to go ahead with this. I told you I wouldn't be gettin married and I'm not. Not to Jeffrey Branson," she sai firmly.

"What about the condominium I bought you on Russia Hill to start your new life and your membership in the Sa Francisco Yacht Club. You're turning your back on a that?"

Carolyn pressed her forehead against the door. Her hea was pounding. She felt like crying. It wasn't just a weddin he was planning for his sister, it was her whole life. Sh wanted to pound on the door, to call out, *let her live he own life.* This was much worse than Carolyn had imagine Much worse than anything her father had ever done. Ho could she have been so misled into thinking he was ju another rich, handsome, well-bred man with a strong wil When he was really a tyrant like no one she'd ever know

"Just watch me," Yasmine shouted and the library do

flew open. Carolyn jumped out of the way just in the nick of time. If Carolyn had any doubts this young woman couldn't stand up for herself, she was instantly reassured. Dark eyes blazing, cheeks aflame, one-hundred-ten pounds of sheer willpower came storming out of the room with her brother close behind her. As Carolyn watched, Yasmine ran up the long stairway, her skirt swirling around her knees, while Tarik stood below glaring at her.

Carolyn knew she had to leave the house immediately. She knew if she left now he might not even know she was here at all. But she couldn't move. She felt as though she ad turned to stone. Shock could do that to a person.

Slowly Tarik turned. He looked like the ceiling had col-apsed on his head, when in reality it was much worse. For im it was his whole world that had collapsed. His eyes vere hollow as if he hadn't slept all night. How long had his argument been going on? Despite everything he'd said, verything he'd done, Carolyn couldn't help the burst of ympathy that filled her heart. He was making a big mis-ake, of course he was. But it was plain he was suffering erribly. Before she felt too sorry for him, she reminded erself what she'd heard him say. How he'd planned to run is sister's whole life after choosing her husband.

"Carolyn," he said, rocking back on his heels. "I'm glad ou're here. Don't go. I have to talk to you. About the edding."

"I don't think there's going to be a wedding. Not after hat I heard...."

"You heard?" he said, drawing his eyebrows together a frown. "Then you know how stubborn she can be. But e'll get over it. Everything will go as planned." His outh was set in a rigid straight line. The same mouth she'd kissed only last night. The mouth that had kissed her with passion and gentleness.

She shook her head. "I can't do the wedding. Not if she doesn't want to marry him."

"It doesn't matter what she wants," he said. "She *will* marry him."

Carolyn felt she was sinking into quicksand. Slowly but irrevocably down, down until she couldn't get out. Just as she used to feel when her father gave an order. She squared her shoulders and pulled herself up and out of the mire. "Not with my help," she said, proud of how steady and firm her voice was. "You'll have to find someone else."

He stepped across the floor and grasped her arm. "Someone else?" he asked. "We have a contract."

"The contract was made in good faith. You never told me Yasmine had refused to marry this man. But you've known all along, haven't you? This isn't a complete surprise, is it?"

"I thought she'd come to her senses," he said grimly "I still believe she will."

"She has come to her senses. Don't you realize that? apologize for listening to your conversation, but I'm no sorry I heard it. Your sister sounds like a remarkably mature young woman for nineteen. I know how much th merger means to you. But I would hope your sister mean more. In any case, I can't be a part of a forced marriage As she says, this is a different world, a different time Women have rights, and she has the right to refuse to marr someone she doesn't love. Let me know if she changes he mind," she said. "Until then..."

She choked back a sob, turned and walked out the fro door. She couldn't stand to look at his face another minut couldn't stand to see the shock and disappointment. He' wanted her support, he'd counted on her support, but she couldn't give it. If he'd wanted her love, he only had to ask. Because it was his and she couldn't take it back. But he didn't want it. All he wanted was for her to help him marry off his sister. That was all he'd ever wanted from her. She couldn't help him.

Tarik walked out the front door and watched Carolyn drive away. Every muscle in his body ached, every bone hurt as if he'd been beaten up by a chain-wielding gang of toughs. Instead he'd only been verbally assaulted by two strong women. He braced his arms against the door frame and exhaled loudly. What was wrong with everyone? Did no one but him see how important this wedding was? Was he the only one who cared about the family?

He heard voices coming from the inside of the house. To avoid anymore confrontations, he turned and circled the outside of the house and entered the garden. He sat on a wrought-iron bench, leaned his head back, and Carolyn's mother's cat ambled up to him and jumped into his lap.

"Thanks, boy," Tarik said, scratching the cat's ears. "I need a friend right now, and you're the only one who seems to understand me. What am I going to do, Max? If I cancel the wedding, the merger won't go through, and I'll let Father down. Not only Father but the whole family who think that money grows on trees." The cat purred softly as if he understood. "But Yasmine's right. I can't force her to marry if she refuses. I only hoped I could convince her." He shook his head sadly. "Women—with their romantic view of life. First Yasmine, then Carolyn, too, the one person I thought would understand. But she doesn't."

While he sat there, grateful for the cat's company, wishing he didn't have to return to the house, or see any one of his relatives, they came to see him. One by one, his cousins, Meera and his aunt all paid him a short visit to give his or her opinion. As if he didn't know what they were going to say.

Yasmine was right, and he was wrong.

He was being overbearing and difficult.

He should cancel the wedding immediately.

Love was the most important thing in the world. Love made the world go round, etc., etc., etc.

After getting his ears full of advice, he continued to sit there all afternoon thinking. What would his father do in this case? What had his father done when he'd refused to follow his advice about love and marriage? He'd simply walked away and let Tarik make his own mistake. Was that what he should do with Yasmine? What would happen if he canceled the wedding? What would his sister do? How could he save the business? When he finally got up from the bench, he realized the fog was rolling in off the ocean and the air was cool and damp. And he realized he had only one choice.

He went to his sister's room and knocked on her door. When she opened it he saw her face was pale and tear-stained. His heart contracted that he'd caused her so much pain. His little sister. The little girl who'd followed him around like a small puppy when she was small, begging him to play with her. She'd idolized him for most of their lives. She never would again, but perhaps they could be friends as peers and adults.

"I'm sorry," he told her. "I was wrong."

She flung her arms around him and hugged him tight. "Tarik, I'm sorry. Sorry I've been such a problem to you. Since you and I are all we have of our family, I wish could make you happy. I wish I could love the man you want me to marry, but I don't. I love someone else.''

''What?''

''I know, I'm only nineteen and so is he. We're not going to rush into anything. I have three more years of school in Lausanne and so does he. By that time...I don't know. I'm serious about having a career, about being independent. The man I love understands this. I hope you will, too. Even more, I hope...I hope...that you'll find love, that you'll believe in its power.''

He couldn't speak. The words he wanted to say were clogged in his throat. Maybe he'd lost the merger, but he'd gotten his sister back. No matter what happened next he realized that was more important.

Dinner that night was noisy and joyous once he'd made the announcement they were all waiting to hear. Though they'd come for a wedding and now there was to be no wedding, his relatives decided to celebrate anyway. Meera outdid herself with a feast served in the baronial dining room, which he rarely used. Tarik looked around from his place at the head of the table, with a vast sense of relief. The look on his sister's face, the color that had returned to her cheeks was enough to assure him he'd done the right thing.

The only thing missing was someone to sit at the other end of the table. A woman who would share his triumphs and tragedies. Someone he respected and admired. Someone to bear his children, to fill this house with noise and laughter. Yasmine would return to Switzerland, the cousins to their high jinks and their school, his aunt to her country and Meera would once again run this house in her own fashion. As for him, he had work enough to fill every day and every evening. Life would go on as it had before he'd stepped into the wedding consultant's shop. Tomorrow he'd pay a visit to the Branson family's office and hope they'd understand. If they didn't...he'd work something out.

He excused himself from the table and called Carolyn. He only got her message machine. He left a brief message telling her to cancel the wedding and to call him. Of course he'd pick up any expenses incurred. Which would be considerable. At this point that was the least of his worries.

The strange thing was that the worst of his worries—the fear that the merger would fall through—failed to materialize. It was as if when he let go of his goal and concentrated on what really mattered—his sister's happiness and her right to plan her own life—everything fell into place. Call it fate, call it providence, call it luck.

First Jeffrey Branson had eloped with his girlfriend. Tarik stood in the Bransons' office when they made this announcement, unable to believe his ears. But it was true. It seemed that Jeffrey didn't want to marry Yasmine any more than she wanted to marry him. Tarik felt as if a huge burden had been taken off his shoulders. If he hadn't been so shocked and surprised, he might have laughed aloud. All his worries—for nothing. So much for interfering parents who all thought they were doing the best for their business and for their children.

The Bransons were very apologetic, so apologetic Tarik was spared the humiliation of telling them his sister had no intention of marrying their son. They had the papers on their desk ready to be signed, hopeful that the merger would go ahead as planned, which would benefit both companies equally. Tarik didn't have to think twice. He signed on the dotted line.

He walked back to his office from the Branson building

The sun was shining brightly on the business district of San Francisco. The sidewalks were crowded with men in suits and ties and women in skirts and high heels. People were talking, laughing, arguing, holding hands, walking briskly or sauntering slowly, but he didn't see them. All he could see was Carolyn's face in front of him, her expression of disgust and disappointment when he emerged from the library after his argument with his sister. If only she knew. If only he could tell her. But she didn't return his calls. Didn't want to talk to him. He couldn't blame her.

When he arrived at his office, and he wasn't quite sure how he'd gotten there—he closed the door behind him, sank into his chair and looked up at the portrait of his father.

"Well, Father, we did it," he said softly. "Yes, *we.* I couldn't have done it without you. Every step of the way felt your hand on my shoulder. The merger will go hrough. Yasmine and I have made up. We will carry on he family traditions, each in our own way. Some day I ope to leave the business to my son and if not..." He choked on the words and couldn't continue. How would he ave a son if he didn't marry? The only person he wanted o marry wouldn't answer his calls and refused to see him. ust because he didn't love her.

Love. What was it? Did it really exist after all? How did feel? Did it make you feel ecstatically happy? If so, he as not in love. He was miserable. He had everything he anted and yet he felt terrible. He'd never felt lonely before nd now he couldn't stand to be alone with only Meera in e big, empty house. He began to spend his days working ntil all hours of the morning, then usually falling asleep the couch in his office and going home to change clothes dawn broke over San Francisco Bay.

* * *

The wedding shop, I DO! I DO!, was busier than ever. Carolyn was glad she was overworked and overbooked. It took up the slack after Yasmine's wedding was canceled. She didn't want to think about it, but she couldn't get it out of her mind. Over and over she replayed the scene at his house in her mind like a discordant tune on a player piano. Each time she did the pain in her chest got worse. The realization that she'd been fooled by Tarik's charm and manners made her feel betrayed.

It wasn't his fault. He hadn't betrayed her on purpose. She had let herself believe what she wanted to believe until she couldn't believe it anymore. She didn't know if she should accept any credit or blame for the cancellation of the wedding. She only knew it never would have worked.

She hadn't returned Tarik's calls because she had nothing to say to him. She was hunched over her computer when the door opened and a breeze blew a stack of papers off her desk. She looked up to see a young woman with dark hair and black eyes and a confident manner that was partly due to her royal status and partly a family trait that Carolyn recognized immediately. It was Yasmine. Carolyn had only seen her once, under the most dire circumstances and her appearance had changed drastically for the better but Carolyn knew it was her.

"Are you Carolyn?" she asked.

"Yes and you are Yasmine."

She nodded, not at all surprised that Carolyn knew her. "May I sit down? I wanted to meet you before I returned to school. Tarik has told me so much about you, how helpful you were. The dress, the ring, even the honeymoon..."

"It was just a job," Carolyn said, hoping she sounded sincere. If it was just a job, then why did she feel so terrible that it was over? "And he compensated me handsomely, so there's no need to thank me. Did everything...is everything all right?"

"Everything is fine," Yasmine said with a smile. "Tarik and I have come to a new understanding. I understand how important the merger was and he..."

"But didn't it get canceled?" Carolyn asked. She'd been aunted by the specter of a failed business deal that she vas partly responsible for.

"No," Yasmine said, beaming at Carolyn. "It didn't. It's long story but it went through just as planned without the vedding. It turned out Jeffrey Branson didn't want to marry ne anymore than I wanted to marry him. But that's not vhy Tarik canceled the wedding. He said he couldn't do t, couldn't force me to marry someone I didn't love. Love. can't believe it, but I think he's coming around."

"Around?" Carolyn murmured.

"To believe in love. The first step to falling in love. If didn't know him better, I'd say he's in love with you. very time he talks about you, he gets this look on his ace."

A flush crept up Carolyn's face. She tried to say someing, to protest that he couldn't possibly be in love with er. She took a deep breath, licked her lips but her mouth as too dry to speak. All she could do was to look down her desk.

"I came today to say hello and goodbye," Yasmine said. I feel like I know you already. I also came to see if you el anything for my brother. He was hurt badly once, and don't want to see him hurt again."

"I would never do that," Carolyn said.

"Good," Yasmine said. She stood and kissed Carolyn the cheek and left the office.

Carolyn sat at her desk staring out the window without seeing anything or anyone on the street. What an amazing girl. What an amazing family. What an amazing man. But Yasmine was wrong about Tarik. She wanted him to fall in love so she imagined it. Carolyn knew better.

But she had to see him. One more time. She'd been rude not to return his calls.

She went to his house the next day. Meera showed no surprise on her taciturn face when she opened the door. Just as she'd done the first time Carolyn had gone there, she showed her in and told her Tarik was in the pool.

Carolyn walked slowly to the glass-enclosed pool where Tarik was doing laps, faster and more energetically than before. Water splashed over the tiles as his muscular arms moved like windmills. She didn't know how long she'd be able to stand there and watch him. Didn't know if she should cough loudly to announce her presence or call his name. Or simply leave and forget the whole thing. She didn't know what she'd say when she got the chance anyway.

Just when she thought she'd give up and go, he pulled himself up and out by bracing his hands on the edge of the pool, his muscles bunching as he emerged from the water. He stood there for a long moment staring at her as if she was an apparition. Her heart banged against her ribs. The memory of that first day came flooding back to her. So much had happened in such a short time. Had she fallen in love with him that first day? She might have fallen in love with his looks, but it had taken longer to fall in love with the whole person.

"Carolyn," he said at last, his voice hoarse and rough. "You came." He stood there in his swimming suit while the water dripped off his broad shoulders.

"Yes, I came to see…I came to say…" What had she come to say? Had she come to ask if he believed in love?

"It doesn't matter. What matters is that you're here. You haven't forgotten me. You don't despise me though you have every reason to. I've been thinking about you, hoping…praying…you'd forgive me for being such a lout, a clod, a boor. I was so wrong, trying to control someone else's life. I thought I was doing what was best for Yasmine, but I was only thinking of business. I thought I knew what was best for her, what was best for myself and for everyone else, but I didn't."

"Then you've changed your mind. At least Yasmine said…"

"Ah, she told me she'd gone to see you. Yes, yes, I had to change my mind when I was confronted with the truth. Love does exist. It's real. And it's painful. Perhaps that's why I didn't want to accept it. But how else can I explain how I feel about you? How lost I've been without you."

His eyes were brimming with emotion, with feelings she'd never seen there. Her heart fluttered in her breast. Could it be…could he really mean what he said?

"You…you've been lost without me?" she stammered, unable to believe his words. Was this the proud sheik she'd heard disclaim the existence of love only weeks ago?

"I thought I'd never see you again. I wouldn't blame you if you refused to speak to me ever again. I was afraid I'd never get the chance to tell you how sorry I am. Can you forgive me? Can you let me court you as a man courts the woman he loves? Maybe some day you'll learn to love me, because I've fallen in love, so deeply in love with you."

Carolyn felt the tears spring to her eyes. At the same time she wanted to laugh. She threw herself into his arms.

He pulled her tightly against his chest and she let the water seep through her blouse just as the happiness seeped into her body. Tarik, the man who didn't believe in love, had fallen in love with her.

"Is it true?" she asked, her voice filled with wonder.

"I only want the chance to convince you," he said and kissed her.

It didn't take long to convince her. Two weeks later after a whirlwind courtship of dinners, lunches, picnics, sailboat rides on the bay, Carolyn was planning her own wedding to the most wonderful man in the world. The richest, handsomest, most thoughtful and most of all, the most loving.

Epilogue

SAN FRANCISCO CHRONICLE

Sunday July 31

The Most Spectacular, Romantic Wedding of the Year

Wedding Planner Plans Own Wedding

Well-known wedding planner Carolyn Evans, who advises clients to allow at least six months to plan their weddings, had only one week to plan her own wedding to Sheik Tarik Oman, chairman and CEO of United Oil Company, in a ceremony at Grace Cathedral. The cathedral, usually booked for years ahead, had an opening due to a last-minute cancelation. That, along with the fortunate and coincidental visit of out-of-town relatives, prompted the bride to disregard her own advice and get married on the spur of the moment.

Ms. Evans wore a white faille taffeta gown with an embroidered ruffle and matching long white gloves. The groom was in the traditional wedding garb of his country. The bride's bouquet was hydrangeas and amaryllis and roses. Stephanotis blossoms tied to the end of each pew filled the church with their fragrance.

The bride's mother, who gave her away, wore a pink satin suit and hat. Out-of-town guests included the groom's sister, the groom's cousins, and aunts and uncles from the Arabian Gulf States. Following the wedding, the newlyweds will be honeymooning on a tropical island in the South Pacific.

After planning so many weddings for others and curing so many cases of prewedding jitters, how did Ms. Evans feel about her own wedding? We caught up with the glowing bride at the reception, which was held in the bucolic garden of the groom's home in the exclusive Sherwood Forest section of the city.

"It was completely different being the bride," she confessed. "Completely and totally wonderful, that is, after I stepped back from being the wedding planner and became the bride. For one day of my life, I was the star of the show, the princess with the glass slipper. Of course my husband makes me feel like a princess every day," she said with a blush.

"The thing to remember is that weddings are about life. About human beings. And emotion. I wanted six months to plan this wedding, to make it perfect, but I took my own advice and remembered that weddings are not about perfection. They're about life which is often imperfect."

"And love," her husband added, pressing his lips

to her hand with the stunning diamond solitaire and the matching wedding ring. "Don't forget about love."

* * * * *